SHOUT-OUT TO MY EX

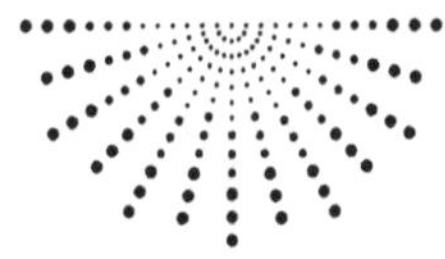

DYNASTEE MCDOWELL

Hardcover ISBN 978-0-9988775-1-8

Cover design by Tyrique Hart

Editing by Imara Vaughn

Ordering Information:

Quantity sales. Special discounts are available on quantity purchases by corporations, associations, and others. For details, contact the publisher.

Orders by US trade bookstores and wholesalers. Please contact:

leah@purposefulmillennialspublishing.com

Printed in the United States of America.

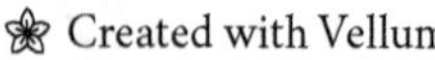 Created with Vellum

Love: One word with a thousand meanings.
These are my eleven.

1

Love – An intense feeling of deep affection

2

Love – Something that lasts a lifetime and brings many requests of you

3

Love – An emotion that overtakes the mind, soul, and body, piece by piece, and then suddenly, all at once

4

Love – A deep feeling that brings endless pain and heartache a toxic feeling that we cannot live without

5

Love – An intense affection that can take control of your mind, body, and soul; a feeling that draws you in just to stir you up inside

6

Love – A life-long lesson that takes you to a place to better you, and bring out a light inside of you

7

Love – A warm, cherished feeling that gives you hope and lightens up the soul

8

Love – An everlasting feeling; to feel complete and whole with the company of someone you call your own

9

Love – A force that attracts you, emotionally and physically

10

Love – A feeling that is built up to break you down

11

Love – Something that must come within or from a spiritual place before it can be projected

PREFACE

Every girl dreams of high school, including me. I dreamed that freshman year would be the start of something new. I would make my own decisions, build friendships, and enjoy all that high school had to offer.

Although I was new on the block, I was ready for everything high school had to offer, including the social life, the long nights studying, and the high school environment.

I was smart, pretty, bold, and ambitious—exactly what I needed to take over the world.

I grew up in house of five. Mom and dad, little brother, and older sister. I was the middle child. My mom would always call me the "fire child" because I wasn't afraid of who I was but, for some reason, no one outside of my family saw me in that light.

I always tried to pave my own way and walk each path I paved with bold confidence but, somehow, I always got stuck somewhere in between being "Domonique's little sister" and "Daniel's big sister." It's hard to be recognized when you're stuck in the middle of two siblings. But no more—I was going to make Eastside High School my own. High school was the place where I would make a name for myself.

And that I did.

By the end of my freshman year, I had definitely made a name for myself and, unfortunately, for reasons that I was not proud of but learned from.

The year I thought would be the best year of my life turned into a series of dramatic episodes that included love, heartbreak, and everything in between.

My life had turned into a never-ending story of what love could do to a person.

This is my story.

CHAPTER ONE

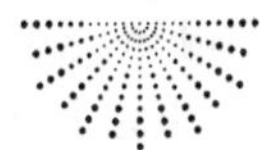

Love – an intense feeling of deep affection

It was the first day of my freshman year at Eastside High School. The excitement that raced through my veins was unreal. I was finally entering a new chapter in my life, a chapter that I would look back on and remember as everything that I could have possibly hoped for in a high school experience. It was "out with the old, in with the new."

New people, new friends, new beginnings.

Everything was going to be great.

On the first day of school, all students received their class schedules upon entering the front doors of the school. I searched for my name on the list labeled "Freshmen" below a large banner that read "Welcome Freshman Class." There was a series of tables lined with teachers who searched through large piles of faintly printed, yellow papers to distribute class schedules.

I maneuvered my way through the crowd to a table that sat in front of a tall pole that had a small sign with "K–O" written across the middle, assuming that each teacher's stack of schedules corresponded to grouping by last names.

"Medina," I said, finally making my way to the table.

"First name?" the man sitting at the table asked as he shifted through the large stack of schedules, never once looking up.

"Denise," I replied.

He thumbed through the papers and quietly read off the names as he passed them.

"You said 'Denise,' right?" he asked, finally looking up from the papers. His eyes were wide and kind-looking. He smiled slightly.

"Yes, sir," I said, looking back at him.

"Here you are, Ms. Medina. Your first class will be on the second floor—that's the English department. If you need any help navigating, all room numbers are posted above the doors."

I took my schedule, nodded a "thank you," and made my way into the large crowd of students who filled the hall.

I walked into my first-period class, head buried in my schedule, trying to figure out what my day would look like. As I lifted my head to scan the room for a seat, I made eye contact with what I thought was the cutest guy I'd ever laid eyes on. Hurriedly, I pushed my hair behind my ears to give it some semblance of neatness, and I ran my hands along my dress to ensure there were no wrinkles. I boldly made my entrance, hoping to catch his eye as I made my way to the desk right behind him.

Boldly, I walked past his desk, stepping over a large black gym bag that read "Eastside High School Basketball, B. Shelton." I took a seat at a desk right behind him, and, as the teacher introduced himself to the class, I couldn't help but think of introducing myself to him.

I mean, of course I didn't know he would become my first love when I walked into first period that day, but, sure enough, he became the first of many to take my heart for a ride.

As I fantasized about the cute movie-like relationship that we could have, my fantasy was quickly interrupted.

The teacher, who had earlier instructed us to call him Mr.

Jacobs, droned on, but I didn't realize that the schedule had shifted.

"I'm Bryant Shelton," the boy sitting in front of me said, standing up from his desk. "I play basketball for Eastside, my favorite subject is . . ."

I daydreamed on.

"Denise Medina."

Tall, handsome, and athletic. Yeah, he's definitely "the one."

"Ms. Medina?"

I wonder if he notices me. He couldn't possibly.

"Medina?!" Mr. Jacobs called.

"Here!" I called back, snapping out of my trance.

"Thank you. Please stand and introduce yourself, Ms. Medina," he said, looking down at the attendance book sitting on the desk in front of him.

"Hi, I'm Denise Medi—"

"Please stand," Mr. Jacobs instructed.

"I rose out of my seat. "Hi, I'm Denise. I love to cheer. I have an older sister and a little brother, and I—" I could hear my voice begin to shake, as it so often did when I spoke in front of large crowds. Or any size crowd for that matter.

I scanned the classroom, and everyone's eyes were fixed on me —everyone except the one person I wanted to look at me.

"And I love to act."

As I stumbled over the rest of my introduction, I slid back into my seat with a sigh of relief. The worst was over.

"Well, it's nice to finally meet you, Ms. Medina." The class giggled. "I actually taught your sister a few semesters ago. If you're anything like her, we should have no problems," he said with a smile.

"Nervous, or nah?"

I peered up from reading the papers on the table in front of me and noticed Bryant turned around in his desk. His dark brown eyes stayed fixed on me as if he were waiting for me to answer what was seemingly a rhetorical question.

"A little," I said, forcing my words past the small lump that had formed in the center of my throat.

Bryant chuckled, his smile showing off his perfectly straight, pearly white teeth. He turned back around in his seat and finished conversing with some guys who I assumed were his teammates as Mr. Jacobs finished reading off the list of names to continue class introductions. As most of the class directed their attention to watch each student who rose from their seat to give their intro- duction and become more acquainted with the rest of the class, my attention stayed on Bryant and what we could be.

He had to be the cutest guy in the freshman class. The way his eyes smiled with his lips. His small, round nose. His coiled, dark hair and athletic physique.

"Why can't he be mine already?" I thought.

The sound of the bell snapped me out of my trance.

With the sound of the bell came the commotion of students gathering their things to go to the next period.

I reached down for my backpack and stuffed my schedule and books from my desk into my bag, attempting to avoid eye contact with Bryant who, to my displeasure, didn't even turn around to look at me before exiting the classroom. My eyes followed him.

"I know you're not checking for Bryant?"

My eyes veered from the doorway to a beautiful, brown- skinned girl with wide, hazel eyes. My backpack was blocking her way. She smiled, looking down at me sitting at my desk, one hand still in my bag.

First period English was not only where I met the love of my life but where I met my best friend, Jalyn Gail Turner.

"My bad, I'll get out of your way," I said, hurriedly zipping up my bag and standing up from my desk.

"It's okay, you're not in the way," she said as we walked toward the hallway, "His name is Bryant. He's on the basketball team, but

I don't see what could possibly attract you to him." She scrunched up her face.

"I'm not sure. Well, I was just looking," I said, stumbling over my words, trying to sound as disinterested as I could muster up the strength to sound. "How do you know him?"

"He went to my middle school. He's cool, but he's not someone to mess around with, get it?" Everything I needed to know about Bryant was told to me by Jalyn.

"Yes? Wait, no. What do you mean?" I asked, half wanting to know what she knew.

"He has some history and, unfortunately, middle school mess just turns into high school drama. I mean it's inevitable, but the best you can do is stay far away from it. That's what I do."

"I mean, he doesn't seem too bad. He seems ni—"

"I'm telling you, girl, that boy is bad news," Jalyn assured me.

I didn't know who this girl was, but boy was I glad to meet her. Something about her was different.

I knew we would be good friends.

For some reason, I felt a trust for her but, even though she warned me to steer clear of Bryant, all I could think about was how I wanted him, and I always got what I wanted.

I took Jalyn's warnings as a challenge because I was capable of changing anyone to be the "right one."

Challenge accepted.

The second bell rang as soon as I walked into the classroom that would be my home for second period.

Once again, we dragged through introductions, and second period rolled right into third.

My third period class was the one I had been waiting for—drama class. Drama class would be a place where I would be open to expressing myself, immersed in creativity with others.

I walked into the classroom and, to my surprise, there he was again.

I scanned the classroom for a familiar face and, realizing that, once again, I was all by myself, I took the seat right next to Bryant.

"Bryant, right? I'm Denise, your future wife," I thought.

In my head, his response would be something beautiful. Something that would seal the deal on our fairytale relationship.

Coming back to reality, I tuned in to what the teacher was saying.

He introduced himself as Mr. Kelly.

"This is Introduction to Drama. We will be acting, but in this class, we will also be completing writing and group assignments. I suggest that you become familiar with your classmates. Get comfortable. Form some good relationships as you will be working with one another throughout the course of this semester," he explained, walking through the rows of chairs that filled the classroom.

I took his suggestions into consideration, but for reasons of my own.

Once again, the bell sounded. This was the lunch bell, and this was the bell that would determine my fate.

See, Eastside High had so many students that two lunch periods were required to accommodate all of the students—Lunch A and Lunch B.

I looked on my schedule, which directed me to the courtyard for the first lunch period. I crossed my fingers and prayed that Bryant and I had the same lunch.

In high school, lunch is not just a meal, it's a social hour, the only time in the school day when there is free reign to socialize.

If we had the same lunch, I would be able to hang out with

Bryant. It would give us the chance to have a conversation outside of the classroom.

But, as I drifted toward the courtyard, Bryant drifted toward Building A, away from first lunch and away from me, and all I could do was watch him walk away. Luckily, I found a group of friends in the commotion that was Lunch A.

I caught up to the group, and we pushed past the crowd, past teachers who were trying desperately to maneuver through the sea of students who flooded the courtyard, past other students who scurried to the cafeteria, and past, what seemed like, a thousand fine-ass guys who shared Lunch A with us.

We filed into the cafeteria and piled plates from the hot line, salad bar, and dessert bar, and made our way back out to the courtyard, finding the first empty table with enough seats for all of us to sit.

Miranda, one of my friends since elementary school, asked excitedly as we sat down, pressing her palms against the table and making sure to make eye contact with everyone at the table, "Did you see all these fine-ass guys?"

"Yes, girl! I don't know how I'll be able to focus 'cause, Lord," Lina added.

And even though this was all true, Eastside High was filled with potential "baes," I had my eye on one, in particular.

"I don't know about you all, but I already have dibs on someone."

Before I could get his name out, from the corner of my eye, I see him walking across the courtyard, but he was not alone.

I looked closer and noticed that this was not just any girl. It was Taylor Jensen—a certified ninth-grade beauty. Her hair was long and dark, and her body was nothing short of goddess-like, mainly because of her long torso and her even longer legs. She was absolutely beautiful.

I had met Taylor over the summer at the mall. We became fast friends. She was kind, and we had a lot in common.

"Hey, what's Taylor doing with Bryant?" I asked, half-knowing the answer to my own question.

"What do you mean, 'what is she doing?' " Miranda followed up my question with another question. The entire table looked at me as if they couldn't understand how I could have possibly not known this important piece of information.

"I mean, what are they doing together?"

"Well, I hope they would be together. They are dating," Lina said as she stuffed a fork full of salad in her mouth.

At that moment, it was over for me. There was no way I could be with him now, especially since he was dating one of my friends.

According to the unwritten girl code, Bryant Shelton was now off-limits to me.

Before I could gather my thoughts after my dreams had been awakened and killed all in the same day, Taylor and Bryant had made their way to the table, adding themselves to the group.

To my surprise, Bryant and I had many of the same friends. We came from the same crowd. I'm sure we occupied the same social settings on countless occasions and never knew it.

One of the many social settings where we tended to gather was the Vista Pointe Mall.

The summer before freshman year, you could count on crowds of students from Lakeshore, Central, and Fairview middle schools to fill the mall on any given day. Everyone who would be attending the local high school from one of the three middle schools first made acquaintance at the mall before ever stepping foot in the halls of Eastside.

It finally dawned on me. Bryant was no stranger. I had seen him before, and it all came back to me. It was a Friday night, and we were all in the open courtyard at the Vista Pointe Mall. I remember walking by a group of boys and one of them commenting, "Damn. She has a big head."

It was in that moment that I hated Bryant, and I didn't even know him.

Vista Pointe Mall was where everyone came together. Where relationships started, bloomed, and died all in the same summer.

~

It was rare that middle school relationships make it to high school, so it was actually a surprise that Bryant and Taylor lasted as long as they did.

A month of our freshman year went by and, soon enough, their relationship came to an end. Somewhere in between sharing English notes and being regular partners for scenes in drama class, Bryant and I became well acquainted with one another.

In the month following the breakup, Bryant and I had become friends. I couldn't see us being anything more than friends. After all, Taylor was my girl. I couldn't find it in my heart to date her ex, especially considering how hard she took the breakup in the first place. What kind of friend would I be? Not only that, but I didn't want people to hate me, and I definitely didn't want to lose a friend over a guy. So I bottled up the feelings that I had for Bryant, and I kept them to myself.

~

It was now September, and that meant "Dating Season" was right around the corner.

"Dating Season" was the time of the year when no one would dare be caught single. With "Horror Nights" at amusement parks and the annual Vista Pointe Christmas Festival being the highlights of the semester's festivities, having a boyfriend was an absolute must. I mean, who wanted to do "Horror Nights" and Christmas alone?

Nobody.

By mid-September, I had my list for prospective boyfriends narrowed down to four. In the entire freshman class of over three hundred students, there were only four guys who I could even imagine myself dating, and I had to get that four down to one by October.

In high school, having a boyfriend wasn't just a coincidence, it was a goal. Just like getting an A in chemistry, getting a boyfriend required hard work, dedication, time, and effort. Most of all, it took a certain amount of choosiness. No one wanted to be with just *anyone,* and no girl wanted the reputation of being with a different guy every month, which was bound to happen if she chose the wrong guy the first time. It was a matter of "do it right, or do it over." Worst case scenario, if a girl chose the wrong guy, she'd have to find another to replace him, and some girls made a habit of choosing the wrong guy over and over and over again. After a while, her reputation would no longer be "the girl with bad judgment," but rather "the pass-around."

And no girl wanted to be known as a pass-around.

A pass-around was a girl who couldn't seem to stay in one relationship for a long period of time but hopped from relation-ship to relationship.

From choosing the wrong guy the first time resulting in singleness to an entire reputation, the risks associated with dating at Eastside made finding a boyfriend serious business.

Even though Bryant wasn't originally on my list, he somehow made his way there.

By October, "dating season" was in full effect and, despite my desperate attempts to not be, I was single.

Every Saturday in October, Scandia "Horror Night" was the regular activity for Eastside freshmen, mostly because we couldn't drive anywhere else. Even though I didn't have a date, I mustered up the courage to go to the first "Horror Night" of the season. Luckily, Ashlyn, one of my good friends, didn't have a date either, so we decided to go together.

Ashlyn and I arrived at Scandia and met up with a group of friends who arrived before us and, to my surprise, Bryant was in that group.

"Horror Night" consisted of haunted houses, mazes, and "safe zones," where people like me could go because they got too scared.

As we walked through the maze closest to the entrance of the park, we were immediately split up, running in terror from actors dressed as monsters and werewolves. I ran to the nearest safe zone, losing Ashlyn and the rest of the group.

"Denise! Why you in there being a baby?"

Dazed, confused, and unable to catch a breath, I looked around to see where the voice came from.

Walking from the inside of the maze toward the safe zone that I occupied was none other than Bryant.

"I am not a baby!" I called back to him.

He came into the safe zone and took a seat on the ground beside me.

"You good, or are you just being a baby?" he asked. "You took off pretty fast. I couldn't even keep up with you," he said, chuckling.

I looked at him. I wanted to be upset because of his lack of genuine concern, but his charm melted my insides. I looked at him with the meanest glare that I could make but, unable to hold it for long, I chuckled.

"Well, come on then. We'll see who the baby is," I answered tauntingly.

We got up, brushed ourselves off, and ventured back into the maze with the rest of the group.

The night was going great and, for the first time ever, I saw a side to Bryant that I had never seen before. He was considerate and nice and sweet. His sense of humor still made him an asshole, but not the complete and total asshole that I had once thought him to be.

As we approached the rear exit of the maze, out of nowhere, a werewolf came running toward us. In a panic, I ran out of the maze and into the park. It seemed as if it had been chasing me forever, and it wasn't until I came around a corner a little too fast, tripped, rolled down a small hill, and stopped just before tumbling into my group of friends that it decided it had had enough fun with me.

I looked up from the ground, and all eyes were on me. I felt like, at that moment, I could die of embarrassment.

Bryant came running down from the top of the hill.

He opened his mouth to speak, but before he could say anything, I stopped him right in his tracks.

"Save your smart-ass jokes, Bryant," I said, rolling my eyes in frustration.

I had made my way to the curb and, as I examined my wound, Bryant made his way to the ground, sitting down beside me.

"You okay?" he asked in the most seemingly sincere tone.

"Yeah, I'm good," I said, smiling and brushing bits of gravel from my knees.

I could feel Bryant watching me as I brushed the dirt from my clothes.

I looked at him again, trying to keep myself from blushing. "I'm good," I said with a slight smile.

He looked at me for a second and, unable to keep his composure, he burst into laughter.

"Good, 'cause you busted your ass!" he said, tears beginning to form in his eyes.

"Fuck off, Bryant! I don't see what's so funny!" I waited for him to stop laughing, but he kept going.

I gave him a slap on the shoulder, stood up, and left to join

Ashlyn with the rest of the group. My night was officially over, all thanks to Bryant.

I approached the group and pulled Ashlyn to the side.

"Are you ready to go?" I asked her, still furious at Bryant's insensitivity.

"Yeah, I'm ready when you are," she said, her face looking confused. "Is everything okay?"

"I just don't want to be here anymore," I explained. "I'm over it."

"Okay, I'll call my mom to come get us."

It seemed like hours that we waited on Ashlyn's mom to pick us up, but that time gave me a moment to reflect on the night's events.

Out of everything that had happened, my mind kept going back to Bryant.

In just one night, I saw the many personalities of Bryant Shelton. I saw his kindness and rudeness. His sincerity and his insensitivity, and, oddly enough, I liked them all.

I never hated and wanted someone so much until Bryant.

Ashlyn's mom finally came and took us home. I was staying with Ashlyn for the weekend.

When we finally made it home, we immediately began to prepare to wind down for the night. We threw on our PJs, opened up our laptops, and logged on to "ooVoo," a video chatting app that everyone used.

I signed into my usual "Hangout" and, not long after I notified the group that I was online, an instant message notification appeared.

" 'BShady' would like to chat."

It was Bryant, and he was trying to send me a message.

What could he possibly want?

Even though Bryant and I were good friends at school, we barely ever talked outside of school and, after tonight, he was the last person who I expected to hear from.

I opened the message. "Tonight was crazy, right?"

Easily, I could've ignored his message, but I didn't want to be rude.

"Yeah, pretty crazy," I responded.

As soon as I hit the "send" button, another notification popped up on my screen but, this time, it wasn't a message, it was an incoming call.

It was then that I had a decision to make. Accept or decline.

Even though he had pissed me off, I wanted to talk to him. I just couldn't help it, but I still wondered what he wanted. We had spent the entire night together, what more was there to talk about? Did he want to get to know me?

I must have taken too long to make my decision, thinking about all of the possibilities of what answering that call would mean, because before I got a chance, Ashlyn reached across my lap and hit "Accept," answering the call.

"Hey, Bry!" Ashlyn said cheerfully, her face taking up most of the computer screen.

"What's good, Ash?" Bryant replied enthusiastically. He was so loud and obnoxious, but that was his charm. I couldn't help but laugh. "Put forehead on the phone."

"Here she is," Ashlyn said, leaning away from the camera and settling back in to her spot on the bed.

I snatched the computer, "That is not my name!" I snapped. "Now, what can I help you with, Bryant?"

"Oh, nothing. I just wanted to see how your knee was doing after that fall."

And this began our conversation that night.

We talked for hours. We talked about school. We talked about life. We talked about music. Movies. Fears and fantasies.

I spoke on the topics, too, but most of the time I listened to him as he told me about basketball and his dreams of making it to the league. As he talked on and on, even babbling at some points, I soon came to accept the fact that a friendship was no longer what I wanted with Bryant.

I wanted more. I wanted him to be mine

Even though the desire to date Bryant was deeply rooted in my heart, my mind screamed "No!" I just kept thinking about his last relationship. I couldn't date him. He was Taylor's ex, and Taylor was my friend, so that would make me a backstabber.

How would she feel if she knew that I was crushing on her ex? I thought. *What would she say about it?*

I let those thoughts go and just continued on with the conversation.

After about three and a half hours, the conversation began to die down.

"It's getting kind of late, and I have to get up for church in the morning," I said to Bryant, attempting to wrap it up.

"You're right," he said. "We should probably get some sleep."

It was late, and I did need to get up for church, but I couldn't help but want to talk to Bryant all night.

After a moment of silence, both of us seemingly unable to hang up, Bryant broke the silence. "Well, I'll talk to you later," he said with a chuckle.

"Okay. Goodnight," I replied, closing my laptop.

My computer was closed, but my mind was wide open. I thought about Bryant for the rest of the night until, eventually, I fell asleep.

We talked on the phone every night. Our conversations were filled with laughter and jokes; we could talk all night, and we did exactly that.

Each night we fell asleep on the phone, and each morning he'd text, "Good morning, beautiful." I'd gaze at my phone screen and blush, attempting to hide my smile under my covers, embarrassed if even the walls of my room found out my little secret.

I was taken by him.

Bryant was funny, sweet, cute, optimistic, adventurous, outgoing, and the list went on. So it was no wonder why I quickly fell for him.

After a while, I began listening to my heart, and I simply let the relationship flow. I didn't care about the consequences.

~

When we got to school on Monday, all anyone could talk about was Friday night.

That morning, my friends were all already at the snack bar by the time I got to school. The snack bar, located in the back of the quad, was the usual meet up place. Every morning, my friends and I would gather at the snack bar for a little socializing before the first period bell.

I walked across the quad and added myself to the group.

I sat down at the table and took out my English notebook but, before I even got the chance to open it, I was rudely interrupted.

"Hey, Denise! How're those knees?" Parker, one of my friends who was sitting on the top of the table, asked.

The entire group burst into laughter.

"The same way your girl's knees feel," I replied.

I was hoping they would forget, but of course with my luck they remembered and had a vivid image of exactly what happened that weekend at "Horror Night."

The bell rang, alerting us that it was time to transition into first period. As I stood up to gather my things, I noticed Bryant out of the corner of my eyes. He made his way over to me and, with a gentle nudge, he gestured for me to walk with him to our next class.

"You look cute today, punk," Bryant said playfully, making me blush faintly.

"I'm always cute—too bad you can't say the same," I replied just as playfully.

"I am delicious, you know. Team delicious."

Bryant was notorious for saying that line, and even more notorious for his flirtatious behavior.

In my head, I couldn't help but agree, but with all of my strength, I tried to look unconcerned.

As I walked through the door of my first period class, my eyes immediately made contact with Jalyn's.

I could see the surprise on her face as she watched Bryant and I walk toward our seats.

I smiled at Jalyn and took my seat beside her, disregarding her expression.

"And what do you think you're doing?" she asked.

I laughed. "Nothing. We just came from the same place, and we have the same class. Nothing serious."

"Yeah, okay," she said, but she and I both knew this was going to be something serious.

Over the course of weeks, between the nightly video calls and daily walks to class, Bryant and I had become pretty close—so close that on October 14th, only three weeks after that first "Horror Night" of the season, Bryant asked me to be his girlfriend.

"Hey, I have to ask you something," Bryant said turning around in his desk.

"What homework do you need? The questions for *Hamlet* or the vocabulary?" I asked. It wasn't unusual for Bryant to come into first period without his homework done, so being the friend that I was, it wasn't unusual for me to give him mine to copy.

"Neither." He reached into his backpack and pulled out a pile of papers. "Already got them," he said matter-of-factly.

"Whoa. Well excuse me," I responded in utter shock.

"Yeah, I know, right? But seriously, I have to ask you something."

I leaned forward in my desk as if he were about to tell me a secret.

"Spit it out then!"

"Well, you know we've been hanging out a lot lately?"

"Yes?" At that moment, I knew *exactly* what he was about to say.

"And," he continued, fidgeting with the imaginary object in his hands, "I really like you."

My heart sank.

"I was wondering if you wanted to be my girlfriend?"

My mind began to spiral out of control. *Did Bryant Shelton really just ask me to be his girlfriend? Was this real?*

He would be my first real boyfriend, but I couldn't say "yes" just yet. I had to clear the air first. I had to talk to Taylor.

Later that day, I found Taylor at lunch, waiting in the lunch line. As I walked up to her, I was pretty sure she knew exactly what I was going to say to her. She was just waiting on me to say it.

"Hey, T. Can I talk to you?" I asked and, even though she welcomed me with a smile and was willing to talk to me, I knew everything was not going to be okay.

I had feelings for her ex, and he had feelings for me, and these feelings were about to turn into a relationship.

I wanted her to hear it from me before she heard it from anyone else.

"Well, you know Bryant and I are super close, and we have been hanging out," I began to explain. I could feel my heart starting to race and my hands getting clammy. "I just wanted to know if you would have a problem with me and him, like talking, or even dating."

In my head, I took a sigh of relief. I had told her. This meant that the hard part was over.

Her face went from bright and welcoming to, seemingly, confused. Staring into space, I stood watching her, waiting to hear her response.

She finally looked back at me, and said, "Denise, Bryant and I were nothing serious. It was a middle school relationship—we are just friends and, if you like him, go for it."

Her mouth said "go for it," but something was telling me that her heart probably said the complete opposite. She encouraged me to date him and encouraged me to be happy with him, but I was still a little skeptical.

I was glad that she gave me her blessing but, for some reason, I felt horrible.

We weren't the best of friends, but we were friends; nonetheless, and I was still breaking girl code.

❧

I told Bryant "yes."

"I'll go out with you, but don't hurt me."

And that was my biggest fear.

We've all seen those movies where the girl falls in love and gets her heart broken, and I didn't want to be *that* girl.

"I promise," he said, and I believed him.

This is where our relationship began.

Before we made it official, we wouldn't dare exhibit any kind of couple-like behavior, but now that we were official, he made it a point to walk me to every class, even the ones we didn't have together, held my hand in the hallway, and showed me off to his friends, introducing me as his girlfriend every chance he got.

Even though I thought this was exactly what I wanted, the newfound attention completely freaked me out.

I couldn't help but think about what people said about Bryant and I when we weren't around. I couldn't help but think about how Taylor truly felt.

But I soon found out.

Not long after we made it official, the whispers began.

"Did you hear about Bryant and Denise? I heard she stole him from Taylor."

"I heard that he had been cheating on Taylor with her all along."

"I heard she is the reason why he broke up with Taylor."

Everyone seemed to have something to say, and everyone seemed to know more about our relationship than we even knew.

Despite the rumors, and the senseless gossip, I was happy with Bryant. He made me happy. We were very different but, somehow, we clicked.

With all the time we had been spending together, the endless conversation, the daily bonding in school, and regular conversations we had throughout the school day, we had become best friends. There was nothing about my life that he didn't know, down to my insecurities and flaws.

Our relationship was the perfect example of opposites attracting. Bryant was a wild child, definitely not the type of guy my parents wanted their daughter to fall in love with, but that just drew me in closer.

Bryant was a troublemaker with a hot temper, and he thought very highly of himself. He made sure everyone knew who he was and what he was working with. His confidence was over the roof.

"Why him?" my mom would always ask me. "What does he have going for himself?"

But she just didn't see what I saw.

My parents weren't the only ones against the relationship.

Bryant's mom hated me. She never said anything to me

personally but, every time I saw her, her dislike for me was written all over her face. Even though she never said anything to my face, I'd gotten a pretty good idea of how she felt about me.

"Why doesn't your mom like me?" I'd ask Bryant.

"It's not that she doesn't like *you*. I promise. It's nothing personal. She just wants me to stay focused on school and basketball. She doesn't want me getting distracted."

"So I'm just a distraction?"

We would have this conversation at least once a week, and Bryant would reassure me that it wasn't my fault the way his mother felt. Apparently, she felt that I was a fast-ass girl in a short-ass skirt, and that's why she didn't like me. I couldn't help but think that, maybe, I just wasn't good enough for Bryant in her eyes. I had no idea why she thought I wasn't good enough, and I couldn't understand why she perceived me as just another "fast" girl.

After we'd both met one another's families, I feared how far our relationship would go, seeing that both of our mothers disapproved of what we had going on. Not having my family's support scared me. My family meant the world to me, and their opinions always weighted out what my heart truly wanted.

Our relationship had run into its first major problem, and it only seemed as if the first problem invited more to come.

I couldn't talk to Bryant because I couldn't let him know I was having doubts, so I talked to my best friend, and Bryant's teammate, Louis Jacobs. Louis was more than just a friend, he was my confidant. If ever I needed to vent or release some frustration, Louis was there to offer a listening ear. We had fifth period together and, every day, I had a new story tell him about me and Bryant. We were probably the most complicated couple that anyone knew, and we had more problems than anyone could understand. But Louis understood, and he gave great advice. He always knew the right things to say and how to say them. Louis was really close to both me and Bryant and had both of our best interests at heart. I appreciated Louis for listening to my complaints because not many would.

"What's wrong now?" Louis would ask. It's almost as if he could sense when I was having a bad day. Maybe it was a natural intuition of his, or maybe the dry tears running down my cheeks would give it away. Whatever it was, Louis was always the first to notice and check on me.

"Bryant and I got into a fight."

"Really? What happened?" he'd inquire.

"He just doesn't get it. He's a real asshole! It's over between us," I'd always say, but never really explain the situation that brought me to tears this time. Yet, somehow, Louis would know exactly how to reconcile the situation.

"Bryant loves you, Denise. And you love him, right?"

"Yeah," I'd say, attempting to keep the newly formed tears from running down my face to make new streaks alongside the old ones from last period.

"Then what's the problem? You guys were meant for each other. You can't let these little arguments come between you. You have to work through your problems."

Anytime we'd have these conversations, I always ended up feeling better, and I always gave Bryant another chance.

Only a month after Bryant and I had made things official, the truth about Taylor began to surface. Apparently, Taylor hated me, and she was genuinely hurt that I was dating her ex.

"Taylor is kind of mad that you're dating Bryant. She thinks you chose a relationship with him over a friendship with her," Jenny Marshall explained to me as we sat in P.E. one morning. Jenny was a mutual friend of Taylor and I. I'd met her over the summer, and we became fast friends simply because we had the same birthday. "She's actually a little hurt," Jenny continued.

It just didn't make sense. She told me to go after him. She even took it upon herself to tell Bryant to be with me, and even more so, she still stayed loyal to our friendship after we started dating. I was so confused.

I knew that if Taylor felt so strongly about the situation, she had to have talked to others about it.

"I'll talk to her," I told Jenny. Even though I wasn't the source of the drama, I wanted to set things straight with Taylor, for both of our sakes. After all, I didn't want to be the cause of our group breaking up, and I could not risk our friendship ending over senseless drama.

After school, I looked for Taylor to talk to her before she went home, but I couldn't find her. It was as if she knew that I was looking for her, so she intentionally made sure that she was nowhere to be found. After looking for Taylor for almost thirty minutes, I decided to just go home.

The car ride home was quiet. I was deep in thought about Tay. *Why didn't she just tell me how she felt?*

When I got home, I fell into my normal afterschool schedule: undress, grab a bite from the kitchen, and log on to social media to see what my friends were up to.

As I scrolled down my Facebook timeline, I noticed something strange about Taylor's recent activity. She'd been posting a lot since school got out and, for some odd reason, all of her posts seemed to be about me.

"When you're supposed to be friends, but she steals your boyfriend."

"Trust no one, even the ones who claim they're for you."

"I'm guessing 'sisters before misters' isn't a thing? *Shrugs*"

My timeline was filled with subliminal messages from Taylor.

She never once mentioned my name, but I had a feeling that she knew I'd get the picture. Still, I didn't understand and, at this point, I didn't want to understand.

If she wanted to be a bitch about the situation, I could be a bitch too. I wasn't going to let her come in between my happiness as far as Bryant was concerned. I wasn't going to let anyone come in between us, for that matter.

The conversation that I needed to have with her couldn't wait, so I messaged her:

"Taylor, I'm not sure what the problem is. I'm not even sure how this problem came about, but if you have something to say, say it to me. This social media crap and the subliminal messages are unnecessary. If you didn't want me to date Bryant, I gave you the chance to tell me, and you didn't. Don't try to flip the story as if I caused all of these problems on my own or as if I didn't care about you or your feelings because I did. The drama is unnecessary and, if you have a problem, address it. If not, keep my name out of your mouth."

Not soon after I pressed send, "Taylor is writing," popped up in the discussion box. I waited anxiously to see what her response would be.

Her message popped up:

"I don't know who told you I had a problem with you, but I don't. We are still friends. It's just weird to see him with someone else. I'm not talking shit about you. I don't know who's putting words in my mouth. I really don't care about you and Bryant. Don't flatter yourself. We cool."

I saw no sense in replying because this was a clear case of "he said, she said."

Even though the air was a little clearer, I did call Bryant to let off some of the steam that had boiled up inside of me.

"Can you believe these girls? They're just mad that they can't find boyfriends, so they sit around trying to ruin everyone else's happiness. They are supposed to be my friends. Why are they being such bitches? I just don't get it."

"I don't know. I wish I could answer that," he said after a few seconds of silence. "But don't worry about those girls. Nothing and no one can ever come between us. Let them hate."

At that moment, I knew I had found the one.

It's a funny feeling when you're in love because it is something that you think is never going to end and something that you will never get over.

"This is a forever thing," we would say to one another.

And just like a rollercoaster, we moved slow, then picked up speed, we had ups and down, sharp turns and loops and, just like every ride, we had technical difficulties and, just like every ride, there was an end, but that did not stop us from riding again.

We know nothing about love at this age, just what we envision it to be: love equals boyfriend and boyfriend equals happiness, something almost every teenage girl wanted and something that I felt lucky to have

CHAPTER TWO

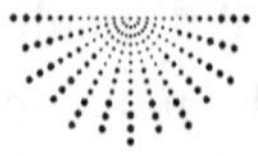

Love: something that lasts a lifetime and brings many requests of you

With every relationship comes requests, and some requests, I just wasn't ready for.

Bryant was a basketball player and, in high school, athletes were the apples of every girl's eyes, especially the basketball players. The Eastside High Hawks boys' basketball team was well-known around the city. They were the best team out there. They had great coaches, and they were three-time state champions. Greatness came from our basketball team and, when girls looked at our players, they saw fame or, in this case, popularity. Every girl wanted to be part of the in-crowd and, by dating a basketball player, she could become popular by association.

Because basketball players were in such high demand in the dating game, landing a basketball player was pretty hard for the average girl, but keeping a basketball player was even harder, considering the requests they were rumored to make.

Something about high school sports drove the typical high school boy to be the overly hormonal high school boy. If anyone was dating a basketball player, most would only assume that their relationship was sexual, but there were exceptions to the rule. Usually, those exceptions had the hardest time keeping their basketball player boyfriends because, even though their answer was "no," there was a long list of girls to say "yes" to any request.

Bryant and I were an exception.

I was a virgin, and I was proud to be a virgin. I planned on waiting until I was married to have sex because I couldn't see myself having sex with the person I wasn't married to. Since I was young, my mother had instilled in me the idea that my virginity was sacred, something that I should cherish. I made a vow to myself that I would wait until marriage to have sex and, in the case that I couldn't wait, I would at least wait until I knew I was in love.

My mind was set—I would not give such a sacred piece of myself to someone unless I *knew* that I would spend the rest of my life with him. So, when Bryant asked, I told him "no." It had only been about two and a half months since we had started dating, and I wasn't ready to have sex. I was only a freshman in high school. What business did I have having sex? I didn't even know how all that worked.

I was very different from other girls when it came to sex. Many of my friends were either sexually active or sexually explorative. I was oblivious to the whole idea in general.

When I told Bryant that I didn't want to have sex, he respected my decision.

"It's okay. I understand your reason. I support it, and I'll stand by you until you're ready," he'd say.

His understanding made me feel warm inside. I knew I had found a good one, someone who was willing to put his desires aside for my beliefs. It made me feel secure, and it made me love him even more than I already did.

~

By March, we had been dating for six months, and things really started getting heavy. Our relationship had been going smoothly, and we were on a good path. I didn't think anything could stand in our way or stop what we had going.

But on March 7th, the course of the day's events would completely change that idea.

It started off as a normal day. I was getting ready for school, and Bryant texted me his usual "Good morning, beautiful."

"Morning," I responded, "can't wait to see you at school!"

"Oh, about that. I won't be at school for a few days. I got food poisoning."

"Really?! I'm sorry," I replied. I felt horrible. He was at home all by himself, and I would be at school so there was nothing I could even do for him. "Well, I'll check on you throughout the day, and I will try to stop by after school."

"You don't have to do that. Really, I'm fine."

"That's what girlfriends are for. I love you."

I was so worried about taking care of Bryant, but little did I know that by the end of the day, I would need someone there to take care of me.

When I arrived at school, I walked up the front gates like I would any other day, but something was different about today. It seemed as though everyone was paying more attention to me, a little more than usual. For some reason, I felt like everyone was watching me, and I heard the small whispers.

"Is that her?"

"Yeah, I think that's her."

It was almost as if everyone knew something that I didn't know. Even though I was confused, I continued with my day and tried not to think too much of what was going on.

Bryant was texting me regularly, making sure that my day was going well, but even his messages seemed mildly unusual.

That day, the hallway seemed longer and more crowded than usual as I walked down it by myself.

On the way to my first period class, I was stopped a few times with questions.

"Denise, are you okay? What happened with Bryant?"

"He got food poisoning." That was my reply for everyone who asked about Bryant and, to my knowledge, that was the truth. But, every time I answered, the person who'd asked the question would either walk away laughing or smile awkwardly as if withholding information that they knew was bad news.

By second period, I was in an advanced state of paranoia. I walked into my science class and, just as they had done the period before, everyone's eyes followed me to my desk.

I could feel my anxiety boiling inside of me.

"What is everyone looking at?!" I snapped.

Only then did everyone direct their attention away from me and become occupied with whatever they were doing.

There was something weird going on, and I wanted to know the truth. I wanted answers. I wanted to know why everyone was treating me as if I were wearing a scarlet letter.

Someone had answers, and I knew exactly who I would have to go to get them—Brenden Reyes.

Brendon was on the basketball team, and he was also Bryant's best friend. I'd known Brendon since preschool, so I felt that I could trust him with giving me the information that I needed.

I marched into my fourth period class, the class that I shared with Brendon, and I went right up to him.

"I want you to tell me the truth," I demanded. "Have you talked to Bryant?"

"Yeah, I talked to him last night," he answered, but his answer was very calm, a little too calm.

"Well, what did he say?" I prodded.

"He just said that he wouldn't be at school today."

I soon realized that I wouldn't be able to get any information out of Brendon. His answers were short and to the point. He didn't say much more than what I was asking him, which was strange because all he ever did was talk. But today, for the first time in his life, he was quiet.

I took my seat across the room from Brendon and, even though the teacher had begun his lecture, my mind was in turmoil, all of my thoughts attempting to answer the question "What in the world is going on?"

Maybe Bryant is dying. Maybe he's leaving me.

I thought the worst.

My interrogation of Brendon didn't go as planned, but I would soon get to the bottom of it.

As the teacher droned on, I slid my phone from my purse and texted Bryant:

"Hey, I hope you're doing okay, but do you have anything to tell me?" I wrote.

Before even having the chance to explain what had been happening to me throughout the day, he assured me that I had nothing to worry about, and I believed him. He had never lied to me before, so I couldn't see why he would start now.

After fourth period, I found my friends at lunch and joined the group at our usual table. Lunch was a wind-down period, so I tried to relax, attempting to clear my mind. It didn't work.

The stares from the hallway had found their way to the court-yard. Instead of simply staring, however, people would laugh and occasionally yell out Bryant's name.

By the time the fourth person yelled out his name, I had decided that I'd had enough.

If Brendon didn't want to tell me what was going on, I knew who would—Dayna, a girl on the basketball team. Since she played basketball, she pretty much knew everything that happened on the boys' team. Between the shared bus rides to and from games with the boys and the automatic connection that athletes had, pretty much all athletes knew even the most sacred "sports gossip," or the gossip about people on the many sports teams at Eastside.

Dayna was close to Bryant but, luckily, she was closer to me. We had a sort of big sister–little sister relationship, so I knew that she'd tell me the truth.

After lunch, just before fifth period, I found Dayna in the hallway at her locker. I pulled her aside.

"What's going on?" I asked. I didn't think I needed to explain anything because, if she knew anything, she'd know exactly what I was talking about.

She took a step back, and her face went from confused to apologetic. The look on her face showed that whatever she knew was nothing good, nothing that I wanted to hear, and nothing that I was going to be able to handle.

"I'm guessing you're talking about Bryant."

I nodded my head with an "isn't it obvious" kind of certainty.

"You don't know?"

"What is it?" My patience was quickly parting from me.

She pulled me further away from the crowd and looked me in my eyes.

"So, after the game on Friday, Bryant was caught behind the school getting head from some girl."

My heart stopped.

"He got suspended, and he may be getting kicked off the basketball team," Dayna continued.

She finished telling me the story, but my mind stopped listening at "Bryant was getting head."

I was shocked. I felt stupid. I was in disbelief. So many things were running through my mind that I didn't know what to do.

My chest felt heavy, and it seemed as if the noise of the crowded hallway intensified. I could hear the laughs, the whispers, and even my heartbeat returning, but this time attempting to escape my chest.

I stood there for a few seconds and, out of nowhere, I began to feel the warmth of tears running down the sides of my cheeks.

"I'm so sorry, Denise." Dayna gave me a hug and disappeared

into the crowd of students shuffling through the hallways to get to their next class.

I stood in the same spot, quietly and, as seconds went by, more tears fell.

I hadn't realized that I'd been holding my breath until I finally came back to reality. In an attempt to regain composure, I let a deep breath out and, instead of air being released from my body, I let out a loud, painful, broken cry. The cry stopped the traffic that was heavy in the hallway. It was as if it were so loud that everyone around me stopped and looked.

In that very moment, it felt as if everyone around me became a part of my personal life. They knew why I was crying. They knew that I was broken. They knew how Bryant was caught behind the school with a girl who wasn't me.

And there I stood—still and unresponsive but totally aware of everything that was going on around me.

Who knows how long I would have stood in that same spot if my friends had been walking down the hall. They quickly pulled me into the girls' restroom, and hands flew toward my face, attempting to wipe the tears that had made streaks of mascara down to my chin.

"What's going on?" Ashlyn questioned as she reached to erase the streams of mascara with fistful of toilet paper she had gotten from a stall.

Still unresponsive.

I couldn't speak. I couldn't gather the words. I didn't want to gather the words. I knew that if I spoke the words out of my mouth, it would make them true, and everyone would know that they were true.

I couldn't speak, so I cried.

Somewhere in between sobbing and trying to catch my breath, I mustered up the strength to speak.

"He cheated!" I cried out.

It was almost as if those two words took all of the remaining strength that I had in me right out of me. I backed away from the wide-eyed, confused-looking girls until I felt the coldness of the bathroom wall on my back. I stood against the wall for a few seconds until my knees felt weak, and then I slowly sank to the floor.

I felt as though my heart had been ripped out of my chest, as if someone that I loved had died.

And someone did die—the honest, trustworthy, caring guy that I was in love with had died, and had been reincarnated as a lying, careless, cheater.

The bell for fifth period interrupted our girls' moment, and my friends hurriedly fixed me up to prepare me for the next class, wiping the tears that were still forming puddles at the bottom of my eyelids and brushing particle of toilet paper from my cheeks.

The five minutes between the first and second bell for fifth period was simply not enough time for my friends to make me look alive again.

Even though I looked a little better, I felt as bad as I looked.

I didn't want to go to class. I didn't want to be seen.

I didn't want to have to face the reality that everyone knew now. The word was spreading around school so fast that they should've just announced with the daily bulletin.

"Are you good?" Mariah, one of my friends, asked, though by my looks, she already knew the answer to her question.

"I'm fine," I said in a whisper. Uncertainty filled my voice.

"You guys go ahead to class," Mariah said. "I'll stay with her."

Everyone filed out of the restroom as Mariah gave one final attempt at making me look as though I had not been hit by a bus. She dabbed my face with warm water, and gave me a tube of lip gloss, probably assuming that it would liven me up.

Instead of taking me to my fifth period class, she took me to Ms. LaCour's class. Ms. LaCour, our French teacher, was the one teacher at Eastside who we knew would understand. She wouldn't just send me back to my class and let me sit there to be to myself.

Mariah stayed with me all throughout the last two periods of the day.

As soon as the final bell rang, I wanted to leave. I wasn't in the mood to hang around the courtyard as I usually did at the end of the school day, but I couldn't call my mom to pick me up from school early. I had no ride home, so I had to walk. Mariah chose to walk home with me to make sure that I was okay.

Mariah soon became my support system through my entire plight.

We walked out of the double doors to the courtyard and walked straight past everyone who was either waiting on their rides home or hanging out until after-school activities started. With urgency, I walked through the crowd of students. I didn't want anyone to see me, and I didn't want to look anyone in the face. I felt so embarrassed. Everyone knew that my boyfriend had cheated on me. My personal life had become public knowledge, and the bad thing about it was that throughout most of the day, I had been trying to take up for him. I had been feeding people the stupid lie that he was at home sick.

As we walked out the front gates of the school, I was still wiping tears from my eyes.

I was home free until I finally lifted my eyes from the ground and saw Brendon standing near the gate entrance.

Suddenly, something came over me. I could not hold myself back. I walked up to Brendon, fist balled, and pure anger and hurt written all over my face.

"You could've told me! You let me walk around looking stupid. You are like my brother! And you let me get embarrassed," I yelled at Brendon.

We stood face to face, tears still rolling down my face.

"You and your friend are dead to me!" I continued.

Mariah pulled me away from Brendon and ushered me out of the gate to begin the long walk home.

And this is where the technical difficulties to this crazy roller coaster began.

~

Me and Mariah walked about thirty minutes from Eastside to my house.

The walk was rather quiet until Mariah finally broke the silence twenty minutes in.

"Have you talked to Bryant?" she asked.

"Yeah, he texted me during sixth period. Asked me why I hadn't been answering his texts."

Who cared if I wasn't replying to his text messages. He didn't deserve a word from me, to be honest.

"And what did you say?"

"I told him that I knew the truth, and that I was done. I haven't talked to him since then."

I finally picked up my head and looked at her. She had a worried look on her face.

"Why do you ask?" I questioned.

She glanced at her phone and slid her thumb down the screen to show me her Facebook. Everyone seemed to be talking about me and Bryant.

I wasn't allowed to have Facebook, but I had one anyways.

I took my phone from my backpack and immediately went to the Facebook app. I signed on and my notifications were blowing up like crazy. I had messages and posts on my wall from nearly everyone.

"Go look at your wall," Mariah said at as I frantically scrolled past notification after notification.

I navigated through my Facebook and clicked on the small icon on the corner of my screen that led me to my wall, or the page in which users could write public messages directly to me.

All down my wall were posts from Bryant.

"I'm so sorry, Denise."

"I didn't mean to hurt you."

"If I could cry and send my love to you, I would to show you how sorry I am."

Bryant's post did little to ease my broken heart. Instead, it turned my hurt into pure anger. No longer was I simply humiliated at school, but Bryant had managed to humiliate me even more, admitting to what he did by broadcasting it all over social media.

It seemed as if I was taking one blow after another, and the day was only going from bad to worse.

I finally made it home.

"Everything is going to be okay," Mariah said, reaching in for a hug.

I gave her a warm smile and allowed her to embrace me. I needed that.

I watched as Mariah walked down the sidewalk and disappeared around the corner.

That day, at that moment, I wondered what I had done to deserve what was happening to me. I began to question myself because I, somehow, believed that deep down inside, this was my fault. Maybe I had asked for this. Maybe if I would've said "yes" just one time, or maybe if I was just a little bit more sexual with him, he wouldn't have resorted to this.

It all made no sense. I wondered, how could the person that loved me so dearly hurt me so badly? And this wasn't just any hurt. The pain that I felt was a pain that made you look in the mirror and not recognize what was there. I felt soulless, helpless, confused.

Even though Mariah assured me that everything was going to be okay, I saw no redemption coming from this.

This was the start of my first heartbreak. This was the start of a changed me, a me I never imagined myself ever becoming, a me that I would never truly understand, a me that would haunt me for the rest of my life.

How could so much go so wrong within twenty-four hours?

It was the longest day of my life. It was as if the world had stood still.

It was life—unexpected. Without warning of what was to come or how it would come.

~

That night I laid in my bed. I felt gray. My room seemed darker than usual, and my blankets couldn't warm me up as they usually could. I lay under my large comforter, and I could feel my face swelling from the tears that continuously dropped.

I turned my phone off that night, so I didn't have to see the constant messages and notifications reminding me of what was going wrong in my life. The notifications were too much to bear.

My thoughts were moving a thousand miles per hour, and as I lay there, I wondered how Bryant felt. Did he feel like his heart just got snatched out of his chest? Did he feel empty? Was he worried, scared, hopeless, and soulless like me? Did he feel the same pain? Did he hurt himself just as much as he hurt me?

I turned over in my bed, and I noticed Brodie sitting in the same place he always was, watching me.

Brodie was the first life-size stuffed animal Bryant had ever bought me. I couldn't sleep without it. Brodie was kind of like my way of having Bryant with me even when he wasn't actually there, even on the nights Bryant and I fell asleep on the phone. Brodie was my Bryant.

I reached for Brodie and dragged him across my bed, but as I moved in closer and held Brodie close to me, I felt something that I had never felt before—empty space.

Rather than comforting me, as it so often did, Brodie showed me exactly what I was.

For the first time ever, I was broken, and I didn't know how to put myself back together.

CHAPTER THREE

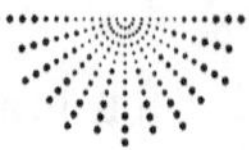

*Love: an emotion that overtakes the mind, soul, and body, piece by piece,
and then suddenly, all at once*

After a sleepless night, there was not much to look forward to the next day.

I opened my eyes, hoping it was all a dream, but as I slid my phone from underneath my pillow and looked at my lock screen, reality set in. My notifications were still buzzing.

That morning, I lay in my bed longer than usual trying to prepare my mind for the obstacles I would face at school.

I unlocked my phone, and a text message notification appeared on my screen along with four others.

"Please talk to me."

"I'm sorry."

"Please, Denise. I am sorry."

I wondered what he was truly sorry for.

Was he sorry that he had cheated on me? Was he sorry that he cheated on me and got caught? Was he sorry for hurting me, making me feel worthless and cheap?

I rattled my brain trying to understand, but I just couldn't see how he could possibly be sorry.

I rolled out of bed and walked to my closet to look for something to wear for school. I finally had gained enough strength to start my morning routine. I walked to the bathroom to clean myself up, but this morning, my daily hygiene routine of making myself look alive was a little harder than usual.

Usually, when I washed my face, the horrid sleep look went away, but not that day.

The gentle splash of warm water on my face seemed to bring out the puffiness and redness of my eyes. It highlighted the redness of my nose after a long night of blowing and wiping.

I finished freshening up, and I got dressed. I slipped into my favorite black comfort sweats and an oversized hoodie. I pulled my hair back away from my face, and I walked to the mirror to examine myself. What I saw was a stranger.

I looked plain and dull.

I had no energy to put on makeup and, besides, there was no point. I knew that whatever makeup I put on would just be ruined because there was no way that I'd be able to hold back the tears all day.

When I walked downstairs, my mom looked at me like she felt sorry for me. She put her hand on my head and pulled me in close, wrapping her arms around me. She kissed my forehead and whispered, "You are strong."

But how strong was I really? Was I strong enough to make it through this day?

My mom dropped me off at school that morning, and I could sense that the day was going to be weird. The sky was blue, and the air was warm, with a faint breeze. The branches that hung over the courtyard bore leaves that were bright and vibrant in color. Everything looked a lot more colorful than I was.

My focus slipped from the beauty of nature to my peers as I walked up the front steps of the school building. I knew that everyone was watching me. If they were not watching me because I was the girlfriend of a cheater, they were watching me because I looked like a walking zombie.

At that moment, I felt as though I would be experiencing another long day.

I pushed my way through the crowded halls, holding tightly to myself as if the thermostat for the hallway was set to freezing, and I was desperately trying to keep warm.

The way a person walks reveals a lot. So I knew that my walk that day showed that I was crying for help.

I felt so alone and hollow inside.

I was early to not just my first period class, but also to every class after that. I figured if no one saw me, then not much would be said, but as I walked through the halls, I still heard the whispers.

"You know, I can't even feel sorry for her. She stole him from Taylor anyway."

"I heard that this wasn't Bryant's first time cheating on her."

"She probably knew that he was cheating."

"She knew better than to date Bryant Shelton. Stupid."

Whether it was a whisper or a full-on bash fest, it was the topic of the day, and people just couldn't get enough of it.

Some spoke down to me, but some sympathized.

"It's okay, Denise. I understand."

"You don't need him anyway. You were too good for him."

"This will only make you stronger."

Even teachers knew what had happened. The teachers that taught both me and Bryant in the same period looked at me in pity. They looked at me as if I was a hopeless puppy. As if they wanted to hug me, whispering words of confirmation that everything would be okay.

But would it actually be okay? I wondered. Would I indeed get through it and be strong like people said I would?

Even though I was encouraged to get better, all I could feel was pain. A pain that stung when you spoke about it, and ached when you thought about it. A pain that dragged you down so low that you feel no way out.

～

Later that day, I learned that Bryant had a meeting with his coaches to discuss his punishment. He had to face the consequences of his decisions, and I wished for the worst for him. I wanted him to feel like I felt, and I knew that the only way that would happen is if he lost basketball.

I stood at my locker in between third and fourth period and, down the hallway, I noticed Bryant walking toward the gym. He peered up the hallway and, immediately, I could see that he had seen me. Everything around me seemed to stop. He glanced up, stared for a few seconds, and fixed his eyes to the floor, seemingly attempting to hide his face, but not before his eyes screamed out to me, "I'm sorry."

His posture was slumped, and he seemed to walk more sluggishly than I'd ever seen him walk. He was usually energetic but, today, he seemed rather lifeless, as if someone just took his soul away.

I couldn't understand. How could he be hurt when he brought this upon himself? He made this decision. He asked for this to happen. How could one be so selfish? I felt as if he had no right to be self-conscious and distressed. At least he got to stay home. At least he didn't have to walk the halls and be reminded that someone that he loved had cheated on him.

I didn't know how I would react when I first saw Bryant again, but now, I did. I was furious.

My anger took control of me, and I lashed out.

I lashed out at the person whom I had deemed the source of all of my problems, who had begun all of this confusion—Crystal Wyatt.

With everyone talking about the situation at school and on Facebook, I'd learned that Crystal was the mystery girl behind the school with Bryant that night.

I hadn't known Crystal prior to the situation except seeing her around school a couple of times. But now, I felt like I knew all that I needed to know about her, and I hated her.

In my eyes, Crystal had no self-respect. No values. She knew what she was doing. She knew that Bryant had a girlfriend. I wondered if her mother had ever taught her how to be a lady.

I wanted Crystal to feel how I felt so, before I knew it, it started. I started the bashing Crystal, and I didn't stop. Whoever would listen, I would tell.

"I heard this wasn't the first time Crystal was caught giving head behind the school."

"I heard she did it to the entire basketball team. What do you expect? That's what girls like her do."

"She only did it to make Brendon jealous because he had sex with her but wouldn't date her."

If I had to walk around school and be called stupid, she would walk around and be called a ho. It was an even exchange in my book. It was the least I could do seeing that she was the pivotal character in the story of how my life turned to hell in only twenty-four hours. I wasn't going to let her get away with it so easily.

And as the rumors about Crystal spread like an airborne disease, I was no longer the center of everyone's eye. Everything began to calm down for me and go to chaos for Crystal.

~

By Friday, the story seemed to have died down. I was happy that the weekend was finally here. Mariah and I had made plans to go to the mall after school on Friday but, still recovering from the week, I simply wasn't in the mood to go.

"Come on," Mariah insisted as we sat in the courtyard, waiting to be picked up after school. "You can't stay in your room all weekend. You'll make yourself miserable."

Even though I still couldn't find the mood to want to go out, what Mariah said made sense. My room was a feeding ground for depression, so I agreed to hit up the mall with her later that day.

I went home, flat-ironed my hair, and threw on an outfit I had bought to wear out that night. Even though I paid close attention to how I looked, looking better than I had in a while, I still felt as though I was dying inside.

My outfit, my hair, and my makeup did nothing to make me feel any better, and as I concealed my pain and hurt with powder and gloss, I looked in the mirror to see all my insecurities staring back at me.

Why was I going out? No one would ever think to be with me after what I had been through. No one wanted a girl with a story —a story that made them look at someone differently.

I was ready. I turned off the light and, as I walked to the front door, I scrolled through my photo album to find a picture to post on Facebook among the many selfies I had taken after I had gotten dressed. I figured if I acted happy that everyone would think I was happy, but it was all a front.

I posted the picture.

I had to prove that I could be something I wasn't. I had to prove that I was okay.

I didn't have any intentions when I went to the mall that night. I just aimlessly dragged along and moved with the group that Mariah and I had met up with in the food court. Most of the people in the group went to our rival high school, Tera Vista High, but I quickly became friends with them simply off the fact that Mariah knew them from middle school. Bryant knew them too; they'd all attended Vista Point Middle School.

I had my guard up since I walked up to the group and the facial expressions changed as soon as they saw me.

Had the news of me and Bryant traveled so far that the students at Tera Vista were talking about it? It was as if my life had turned into a reality TV show that everyone was tuned in to.

Mariah and I added ourselves to the group. The conversation was normal. They were talking about the upcoming basketball games, parties that we had planned on attending, not much of anything interesting. I let my guard down when I realized that the weekly gossip had not come up in their conversation.

But I let my guard down too soon.

As we walked through the mall, we ran into another one of our friends, Reggie. Reggie was notorious for his wild humor and goofiness. He greeted us with a cheesy smile, calling us by the silly nicknames he had given us.

"My, oh, Mariah. Where have you been?"

Reggie was Mariah's cousin.

We all laughed at the comedy routine and, as we laughed and carried on, my laughter was brought to an abrupt stop.

"Yo! Who got caught behind the school getting head? I heard about it on Twitter!" Reggie said with interest and amusement.

It was at that moment that I realized that my situation was a kicker, something that sparked laughter in peoples' everyday conversations.

Mariah's eyes widened, and she looked at me from the corner of her eyes to see if I had reacted to the joke.

But before the conversation got awkward, I quickly replied. "You would never guess who it was, Reggie. It was my dumb-ass boyfriend, Bryant, and a fat bitch named Crystal."

As the statement fell from my mouth, I fought to hold back the tears and topped my sarcastic reply with a sweet smile and a chuckle to lighten up the awkward silence.

"I'm so sorry," Reggie said, seeming to realize that he had stuck his foot in his mouth.

"What do you have to be sorry for, Reggie?" I laughed. "It's not like you're a cheating sex addict."

The words I spoke were brutal. The words I spoke were mean, but they were nothing short of the truth and nothing short of how I felt inside.

Then came the question.

"Are you okay?" Reggie asked with a concerned look on his face.

I wanted to scream to the word "No!" but I had to keep up the act.

I smiled, looked Reggie dead in the eyes and, with confidence and certainty, I said, "Yes."

This was the first lie of many to come.

Mariah looked at me with a confused look on her face, as if she couldn't recognize me.

How could I be okay when I was crying throughout the night and beating myself up inside? How could I be okay when I couldn't fully grasp the reality that my boyfriend had cheated on me? How could I be okay when just hearing the name "Bryant" sent me straight to tears? The answer was "I couldn't possibly be."

But that night, whether they believed it or not, I was okay, and I was going to be okay.

That night, I made sure I talked to different guys, and I even gave my number out. I was single, and I was going to show everyone that I could bounce back. I was strong, and I was resilient, and I was a firm believer that it was Bryant's loss and not the other way around.

I looked strong and acted strong but, in reality, I was getting weaker by the second.

I couldn't help but think about Bryant and what he was doing. I wondered if he was thinking of me too. I wondered how he was feeling and if he missed me and wanted to talk to me as badly as I wanted to talk to him.

Even though he hurt me, I wanted him in my presence because, at one point, he had made me feel so good. I wanted my boyfriend back. I wanted this pain to escape me, and I wanted everything to go back to normal.

I didn't completely shut Bryant out, but I did give him the cold shoulder. I was a total bitch to him, and he definitely deserved it. I thought being mean to him would bring me some closure, would make me feel better, but it did nothing to ease my aching heart. I was going out of my way to do things that were out of my character.

Before Bryant, I was a bowl of sunshine. I was happy, energetic, unbothered, and innocent in a way. But now, I couldn't understand what or who I was. I couldn't understand what was wrong with me or why I couldn't go back to normal. I didn't like who I was becoming.

Bryant was scheduled to come back to school that Monday. I realized that I would eventually have to talk to him about the situation, but I didn't want to. I didn't want to know. I knew that hearing the story come from his mouth would hurt me even more, and I wasn't ready for that. I could barely deal with the pain that I had already experienced. But I knew it had to be done, and I needed to get it over with once and for all.

I waited for Bryant outside of first period. I wanted to get the conversation over with especially being that I would see him throughout the day because we shared several classes. It felt as if I had been waiting for hours when I finally saw Bryant towering over the flood of students that crowded the hallway. Immediately, his eyes locked with mine.

"We have to talk," I said as he approached the classroom door.

He nodded his head in agreement but didn't say a word.

When the conversation first started, I didn't know what to say, so I asked the one thing I really didn't even want to know the answer to.

"Why? Why did you do it, Bryant?"

Before he even had the chance to respond, I had already come up with every possible reply that he could have had, but my imagination was soon drowned out by his dull, flat answer.

"I don't know," he said with seemingly no emotion.

My mind went into a frenzy.

" 'I don't know?' What the fuck do you mean, 'I don't know?' " My voice had gotten louder, causing a few stares. "You cheat on me, and you don't know why?"

I was infuriated and fed up with him. He was so thoughtless and callous that it drove me off my rockers.

"Did you even think of me when you decided to do it? Did you forget you had a whole-ass girlfriend?" My voice began to quiver and, suddenly, I could feel the bottom of my eyelids get heavy with water.

"How could you, Bryant? How?! I was everything to you. I would do anything for you. I did right by you. I was willing to give my all to you, Bryant. What did I do wrong? What did I do to deserve this treatment from you?"

The questions fell from my mouth like loose teeth but, honestly, they were all rhetorical.

I didn't want to hear his answers. I didn't want to hear his explanations. I didn't care.

He stood there in silence, a silence I could not bear to hear.

He stared at me with a hurt look on his face, and I stared back at him in confusion. How could he have nothing to say? He couldn't have expected me to feel sorry for him.

I was angry, not because I hadn't gotten the answers to my questions, but because I had cornered him, and he did nothing to defend himself.

I walked into the classroom feeling no better.

I hated Bryant, but it wasn't for cheating on me, it was for not fighting me. It was for not fighting for me.

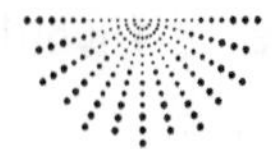

CHAPTER FOUR

Love: a deep feeling that brings endless pain and heartache; a toxic feeling that we cannot live without

Vincent van Gogh is famous for the color and emotion of his paintings, which speak to people, give them life. But, even though he was a great painter, he was physically and psychologically unstable. His yearning for happiness and positivity may have led him to an addiction—eating yellow paint. Even though the paint was toxic and harmful to his body, he ate it anyway.

Yellow—such a bright, warm color. The color of the sun and sunflowers. The color that symbolizes peace and happiness.

Bryant was my yellow paint. Even though I knew he could not do right by me, and he didn't care for me the way I cared for him, even though he mistreated me and was unkind to me, I let him back into my life. After Bryant cheated on me, I found myself drawing back to him. I just couldn't let him go.

The truth was, I yearned for this toxic relationship because I thought he was the source of my happiness. I thought that there was no way I could be happy without him. He was like a drug—he was bad for me but, at certain moments, he made me feel good.

He made me into a person that I didn't understand and, just like the yellow paint, I let Bryant intoxicate my life.

Deep down, I feared starting over. I feared taking chances, stepping outside of my comfort zone. I didn't want to start over with someone new. I was scared of opening myself up to another person. I was scared of someone taking advantage of my heart again, so I stayed with the one who had already hurt me. I figured that it couldn't get much worse. I would tell myself that there was no way that he could hurt me more than he had already.

After his constant begging and pleading for another chance, I gave him one. He seemed as if he knew he made a mistake. In the eyes of my friends, I was being stupid, but I just didn't want to give up on love so easily.

At the time, I didn't realize my worth. I was so caught up in having the dream relationship that I saw in the movies that I was completely oblivious to what was actually being done to me.

I believed that people could change. I believed that people learned from their mistakes, and I believed that Bryant and I would never enter that dark place again. He was so persistent in his attempts to prove that he was sorry, that he had changed, that I saw no reason why he would cheat on me ever again.

"Everyone deserves a second chance," I thought, and I gave Bryant that second chance.

Our relationship was rekindled and, even though I didn't completely trust him, I knew that one day, it would get better. One day we would rebuild what had been broken.

By mid-sophomore year, Bryant and I were a full-fledged couple again, but I still had not gone back to the girl I once was before my heartbreak. Freshman year, I had lost my boyfriend, and even worse, myself. I was a changed person. I went to parties. I started drinking, and I became quick-tempered.

I came into sophomore year hoping for a change.

I didn't make the cheer team sophomore year. But sophomore year, I found my own way without cheer and became heavily involved in my academics. I made myself more active and took part in clubs and sports, looking for a way to express myself freely. I started to write more, and I advanced tremendously in my drama class.

Mr. Kelly, my drama teacher, encouraged me to write down all of my pain, struggles, and misfortunes. He pushed me to connect with my monologues and scene work by acting out what I was feeling on the inside. This newfound means of expression was refreshing. It gave me relief and, even though I was back with Bryant, I didn't spend as much time as I used to with him. We had rekindled the connection, but I had managed to cut off the attachment.

I had found my independence, and I was making a name for myself that didn't have a negative story attached to it.

You would have thought I was getting my life together, and everything was on track.

I felt like I could only go up from there, especially seeing how low I had been.

Bryant and I were not perfect. There were days where I openly blamed him for the way I was—closed up, defensive, and even a bit pessimistic.

I never let him live down what he had done. I thought that I had forgiven him, but I simply could not forget.

Some nights, we would just sit on the phone in silence. Sometimes I would ask "Why?," half-expecting him to give an answer this time, but he never did. He never wanted to talk about it, almost as if it were something he was trying his hardest to forget.

I would start arguments for no reason and pick fights over the smallest things.

"Who was that girl who commented under your post?"

"What took you so long to respond?"

I had become a jealous, controlling, insecure girlfriend that needed to know *everything*.

Bryant and I continued our up-and-down rollercoaster of a relationship that was getting unhealthier by the day.

We argued often and took pride in saying hurtful things to one another. I said unkind things to him, but I knew boundaries. He, on the other hand, had no remorse for the words he would say. He was so blunt and harsh and, when it was pulled out of him, he showed me that he could break me down and tear me apart with one sentence.

I would push him. I wanted him to say what he really felt inside. I would get under his skin just to hear him say how he really felt, even if it did hurt me.

We became hateful toward one another. We would argue just so we could kiss and make up.

Our relationship was toxic, but we kept it going, despite opposition from others, and even despite our own good judgments.

"Why are you still with him?" my friends would ask. "Why do you deal with all of the drama that he brings into your life?"

I never really had an answer to these questions.

I knew Bryant hadn't changed. He simply got smarter with how he cheated. He slept and pleasured himself with multiple girls, some I knew and some I didn't.

Even though I remained loyal, I wasn't giving him the sexual pleasures that he wanted, so I reasoned with myself. I thought it was only fair that he got it from someone else.

My logic was messed up.

I made excuses for him. I let him take advantage of my openness to allow him to explore other girls, and he knew that no matter what he did, I would always be right there with open arms willing to take him back.

~

Throughout that year, I stayed in the relationship with Bryant, but I did have suitors. The majority of them were guys who expressed their interest in me, but I could never focus on them because my mind was still on Bryant.

But I did have friends.

That year, I made a new friend named Johnny Carter. Johnny was on the football team. He was quiet and shy. He wasn't an everybody person but, once I got to know him, I realized he had an amazing personality. He was a great friend, and a good listener.

We became friends at the beginning of my sophomore year, but I liked him a little more than a friend. Johnny and I immediately clicked but, because of my relationship with Bryant, I ruined all chances of me and Johnny being more than friends. Johnny made it quite clear that he wouldn't pursue me intimately because he could see that I was still very much in love with Bryant.

That year, Johnny transferred from Eastside to Vista for a better opportunity in football. We stayed in contact and became even closer friends.

By spring break, Bryant and I had become more distant than ever. He was always too busy for me. He seemed very uninterested in being part of my life. I couldn't understand what I was doing that was pushing him so far away from me. Our conversations became short, and the time we spent together no longer existed. It was as if we were no longer together, but neither of us had ever said it.

Spring break was also when I noticed Bryant's postings on Twitter.

One night, I had noticed a string of posts on Bryant's page that all pointed to some girl. They were intimate and heartfelt, but I soon came to realize that they weren't for me.

After much investigation, scanning his page to find consistencies in the users who liked his posts and pictures, and who frequently commented on his status updates, a girl named Dedra became the prime suspect.

I went on to investigate Dedra's Twitter activity, and her posts were strangely similar to his. They had managed to have entire conversations using nothing but subliminal messages, and their messages pointed to a relationship.

As I sat back in my desk chair, I tried not to overthink the situation. I tried to give Bryant the benefit of the doubt because, though all the evidence lined up in theory, in reality, I had no idea of who the girl was.

Her Twitter bio read that she lived in Las Vegas, so I wondered how Bryant could possibly be dating someone who lived so far away. I reasoned that the girl Bryant had been conversing with online could not have possibly been anyone serious, and I managed to clear my mind of the situation.

I thought.

Throughout the entire week following my investigations, I couldn't get the Dedra girl out of my head.

One day, I couldn't bear thinking about it anymore, so I asked Bryant straight up.

"Who's Dedra?"

It was almost as if my question had taken him aback.

"Dedra who?" he asked.

"The Dedra who is liking all of your pictures, and commenting under your status updates. That Dedra."

"She's just a close family friend. We grew up together," he explained, and that's all I needed to hear.

I breathed in a sigh of relief and released the confusion and frustration that I had bottled up inside of me. I was worried for nothing, but who could blame me? I was in love with someone who saw no harm in constantly hurting me. I had probable cause.

~

Days went by after that conversation, and Bryant spoke to me less and less. On some days, I wouldn't hear from him at all.

I let my investigation of Dedra die down, but I soon came to find out that Bryant hadn't told me the entire truth about her.

As I lay in my bed scrolling down my Instagram news feed, a picture caught my eye. The picture was of a beautiful, bright-faced girl, with long hair full of curls. She had a warm smile on her face as she rested under Bryant's arm, leaning into his chest. Bryant had posted the photo. Bryant's smile was warm, too, a smile that I hadn't seen in a while.

I looked closer at the picture and realized where they were. They were in his room lying in his bed.

I studied the picture and soon came to realize that the girl was Dedra.

"Happiness." I read the caption to myself. The word was followed by red hearts and kissy-face emojis.

My mind went into a frenzy.

What is this? Why is she at his house?

Questions that I truly didn't want to know the answer to filled my mind.

I screenshotted the picture and sent it to Mariah; not soon after, my phone rang. I answered immediately.

"Whoa! That's some crazy shit!!" Mariah yelled through the phone.

"I know, right! He is one bold asshole!"

"This is crossing the line. No going back from here," she said as I reread the one-word caption, still trying to make sense of it all.

And she was right. He had gone too far.

This showed me that he didn't have a sense of care concerning me.

"He takes joy in making a joke of me, embarrassing me, making me regret every decision I made regarding being with him," I thought.

"Hold on, Mariah. I have to call you back," I said, hanging up the phone.

I scrolled through my contacts and called Bryant.

No answer.

I called him again.

Still no answer.

I must've called him a hundred times before figuring out that he probably didn't want to speak to me. So I texted him, but he didn't respond.

I lay back in my bed and examined the picture, still trying to piece it together in my mind.

As I read through the comments, a text message notification popped up on my phone screen. I clicked on the message to open it, and my heart sank.

"I don't want you! I don't want to be with you! You can't do anything for me!" I read aloud as tears began to well in my eyes.

His words played over and over in my head. They ate at my soul and made me insecure inside. How could he say such dreadful words to me? How could he have such a strong hatred towards me when, just a week ago, he loved me?

After a while, I stopped focusing my attention on what he had done and started thinking about what I had done. How did I let myself go through this again?

At that moment, I wanted to know everything. There had to be more to the story. Why did he just up and leave so quickly? How long had he and Dedra been a thing?

Unable to answer the questions myself, I went to the only person who I thought would answer them—Dedra.

I found her page on Twitter and sent her a message.

"Hi, you don't know me, but if you don't mind me asking, what is your relationship with Bryant?"

And just my luck, she replied.

"Bryant is my boyfriend."

"Really?" I replied, "How long have you both been dating?"

"We've been dating for a couple of months, probably three."

She went on to tell me about how she was from Vegas and how she was in Cali vising him. Apparently, she had family in Cali, and she had been visiting frequently.

Everything added up. Everything started to make sense.

Bryant had been neglecting my attention and blowing me off because he had been dealing with Dedra. He had lost interest in me because he had gained interest in someone else.

After answering my questions, she'd finally gotten around to ask me who I was.

"I'm Bryant's ex," I told her.

I let her know that while he was with her we had an ongoing relationship, a two year "on-again-off-again relationship."

"But it's over now," I explained. "I see that you two are happy together."

Her next messages threw me off though.

"Well, it's about time he got something real in his life."

She proceeded to say that I would never be able to keep a man because I was weak, because I let someone take the one I had so easily. It hurt me. But I was no weak chick. I let her know it was fine, and that she could have Bryant and all of his cheating ways. I wished her the best.

"Remember," I said, "no matter what you give him, I kept him as long as I did giving him way less."

I closed out of my Twitter app but, instead of crying, I sat in my bed in silence. I was tired, my head was hurting, and my mind was racing a hundred miles per minute, but I couldn't sleep.

I tiptoed downstairs and went into the cupboard to find some pain relievers. I opened a bottle and took two 800mg painkillers and a sleeping pill. I just wanted something to knock me out for the night. I poured a glass of milk, scarfed down the three pills, and returned to my room.

As I lay in my bed, I could feel my body getting drowsy and my arms and legs starting to tingle. My limbs became numb, and it felt amazing. Slowly, my body drifted off into a deep sleep. It was the best sleep I had ever had. For the first time in weeks, I could go to sleep with no problems, and I didn't wake up in the middle of the night crying. I didn't toss and turn. I was at peace.

~

At this time, my mom knew very little about my personal life, not because she didn't care, but because I didn't think she needed to know.

My mom was the type of mother who showed no sign of weakness. She was strong and independent, and I felt that if she knew how weak I was she would judge me. I always felt as though I had to be just as strong as she was. I couldn't cry over small things like relationship problems and rumors. I had to push through.

I loved my mom. She was absolutely amazing, but there were some things that she just didn't need to know about me. So I always put on a front that my life was good.

"So, Denise , how are you feeling?" my mom would ask after she found out that Bryant and I had broken up.

"What do you mean? I'm as good as I've always been. No love lost."

My answers were always sarcastic. I even began to make a joke out of it as if it never bothered me.

"His loss, not mine," I'd say, but my mom saw right through my front. She could see that, in actuality, I was weak but, luckily, that's all that she saw.

I became dependent on medication to help me sleep after the

first time. Every night, I was taking over-the-counter sleep medication to get me to that peaceful place that I first experienced and, every night, it took more and more doses to get me there.

And that's where it all started—first it was just for sleep, then it was just for headaches or muscle aches. Even though I liked the feeling, I knew that I couldn't get hooked on medications, so just as soon as I started, I stopped. I figured I'd rather fight trying to sleep than have to fight an addiction.

It took me a while to notice that though I'd stopped taking pain pills, I was still battling with an addiction, and that addiction was Bryant Shelton.

After the Dedra situation, Bryant apologized and, once again, I forgave him. We got back into a relationship at the end of my sophomore year, but the new relationship didn't bring about new behaviors. The same verbal and emotional abuse that plagued our relationship before was still very much a part of our new relationship.

The same darkness that loomed over me for much of my freshman and sophomore year was not going to follow me into junior year. However, I didn't let it affect me as much. I was still an honor roll student. By the end of my sophomore year, I had gotten back into cheerleading, I even made varsity, and I was the newly elected Junior Class Vice President.

My honors and accomplishments had "successful" written all over them, but inside I was dying.

When Bryant and I weren't together, I found myself begging for him back, begging to be with him and going against myself just to try and have him back. He'd, of course, take me back, but the emotional neglect that I felt with him would continue to tear me down.

The heartache had become so unbearable that I no longer wanted to live. I knew that if I were gone, I would no longer be sad. I would no longer have to deal with pain and hurt. I would never have to cope with another heartbreak.

I had spent two years telling myself that I was getting better, but I came to realize that this was a lie. The only way I knew was out.

I figured that if I took one too many pills, I wouldn't have to wake up and deal with the hurt anymore. The thought of leaving this world seemed more inviting than life did and, even though everyone saw me as happy, my world was darker than it had ever been.

Depression was like a war, and I was either going to win or die trying.

I did not choose to be like this, and I didn't know how I got to this place, but I didn't want it. I didn't want this to take over me. I needed to find a way out.

I was forcing all this yellow paint down my throat, hoping for a change but not realizing that, in due time, I could be gone forever if I believed that this yellow paint would make things better and make me okay someday. This paint was intoxicating, it was taking a toll on me, pushing me away from my faith. I never let anyone know about my darker days. I never really saw it in me to share the state of mind it put me in. I felt people wouldn't look at me the same if they saw all my scars, if they knew all the pain I went through. My smile was capable of hiding all my pain; I hid my issues with a smile. I smiled like I was truly happy. I smiled like nothing in my world was wrong.

CHAPTER FIVE

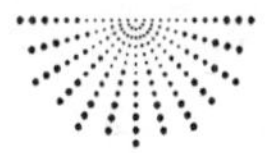

Love: an intense affection that can take control of your mind, body, and soul; a feeling that draws you in just to stir you up inside

I took on a challenge to find myself and to get myself back. I was tired of being ashamed. I cleared my mind of all negative and suicidal thoughts. I cleared my mind of the toxic relationship that I had with Bryant. I put my best foot forward and started focusing on the things that really mattered.

When I began focusing on positivity, I invited positivity into my life, and that summer turned out to be one for the books. That summer, I took a completely different path than what I was used to. I partied, I drank—I had turned into a "rebellious teen."

Most of my days were spent hanging out with friends. I went out more. I laughed more and, for the first time in almost three years, I was living a single life. I had no worries and no problems.

This was the summer I established a circle of people I would later consider my best friends.

There was Jayln, Briana, and Hunter.

Briana and I became friends mid-sophomore year after choosing one another as partners for a dialogue read in drama class. Briana was loud, free-spirited, and strong-minded. She was kind of a handful, and she encouraged me to be the same way. She encouraged me to be unapologetically vocal and mentally free, and I was when I was around her. She brought out the bitch in me.

Briana and I had a lot in common, including similar relationship situations. We would talk about our exes, and I would find comfort in knowing that I was not alone. We made a vow that no guy would be able to take advantage of us ever again.

Hunter was my go-to guy. We met in 6th grade and had been inseparable ever since. I always thought of Hunter as the older brother I never had. He was protective, quiet, and kind-hearted.

That summer, Briana, and Hunter helped me find the person that I thought I lost—myself.

While new relationships were growing, old relationships were being resurrected.

Bryant reached out to me several times over the summer, and we remained in contact.

I forgave Bryant for everything he had done to me, realizing that we were all young, that we made mistakes in our youth, and I moved on.

We were better off as friends, but I still loved him. I cared for his well-being.

The truth of matter was that I was incapable of holding true hatred towards someone. No matter how much I would say it and how strongly I would express it to my friends, I never really hated Bryant. In my world, "I hate you" is the strongest "I love you." I would scream out "I hate you!" to cover the fact that I had nothing but true, unconditional love for that specific individual.

That summer, I found myself becoming friends with several different guys, but I remained single, even throughout junior year.

I flirted with guys, went on dates, and enjoyed the attention I received, but I made sure I let them know I wasn't ready for anything serious. I was guarding my heart because I did *not* want to be hurt again.

~

I focused on school, friends, and personal development my junior year. I was still heavily involved in drama and had begun writing again. I was now in the Drama Two class, which allowed me to focus on my writing and developing my monologues.

Every year, the Drama Two class hosted "Ten in a Black Box," in which students wrote ten-minute plays and had the opportunity for their works to be presented in front of an audience. Though I had little faith in my own work, Mr. Kelly encouraged me to enter my play.

Mr. Kelly was my biggest supporter when it came to the teachers at Eastside. He always pushed me, and he knew I was destined for greatness. He knew that I had a story that needed to be told, that needed to be heard.

I went home that night and started writing. I titled the play *Dumbfounded in Love*. It was a play about my relationship with Bryant and the dynamics of high school and friendship. This play was based on a true story; it was very personal, very raw, and relatable. I knew I couldn't be the only one that was affected by a relationship, and I knew I wasn't the only one who had drama with friends, issues at home, and insecurities inside their heart.

Not only did I write the play, but I was cast in it. This would be the first night that my work and my acting talents would be seen before a large audience. About half the student body, families, and friends were in attendance, and I was extremely nervous. The nerves soon went away when I got on stage. The adrenaline that rushed through my veins seemed to fuel my confidence.

My play ended and received a standing ovation.

Following the event, attendees filed into the foyer outside of the theatre.

As I stood in the foyer searching for my family, I could hear people talking about the show, my play in particular.

They loved it! My play was a success.

It was then that I realized that my **pain** had a **purpose**. Secretly, I thanked Bryant because if it were not for our relationship, I would not have had a story to tell.

The play was not only for entertainment, but it was to tell the story of my struggle, and it did just that. For the first time in a long time, I truly felt proud of myself.

That year in high school I realized that I was capable of being okay.

CHAPTER SIX

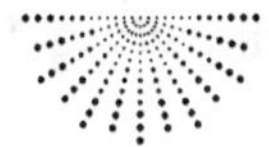

Love: a life-long lesson that takes you to a place to better you, and bring
out a light inside of you

By senior year, reality was setting in. I had entered the final chapter of my high school story, and I was ready to make the best of it.

I had become the varsity cheer captain. I had earned a spot on the executive student council, and I'd sealed my spot as a member of the Advanced Drama Department. Coming into my senior year, I was determined to make it the best year of my life—no more boy drama, no more girl fights. It was just me and my best friends. My senior year was all set, and I was ready to take it on with amazing people by my side.

Coming into senior year, one of my good friends from middle had transferred into Eastside. His name was Cameron Gonzales.

In middle school, Cameron, Hunter, and I were "the three amigos." Hunter and Cam had been best friends since elementary school; I was added on later in middle school.

Cameron had always been a friend to me, but somewhere in between Sunday dinners as a group with Hunter, Bri , and I, and evening study sessions, I had become interested in Cameron as more than a friend.

I had always found him to be beautiful. He had a warm smile, with dark black hair that was always wild. He was tall with hazel brown eyes, and had a warm smile that made me melt inside.

My crush on Cam was something that I kept to myself because I didn't want to potentially ruin a friendship. I didn't want to make things weird over a silly crush. We were going on six years of friendship, and I didn't want anything to come in between that. Our relationship remained platonic, but he sure did become an important part of my life.

~

One Sunday, I invited Mariah, Briana, Hunter, and Cameron over for a small cookout. My sister and I slaved over the stove to make sure that the food was just right. She made the macaroni and cheese and, even though she tried her hardest, her mac and cheese tasted like ass and cheese.

I stuck to what I knew and made the baked beans and my famous corn bread.

When the food was ready, we all gathered in the kitchen, made our plates, and took our seats around the dinner table, quietly— the first time it had been quiet all night. The only time it's quiet in a black person's house is when they are eating or sleeping, and this was one of those times. Everyone had their face first in their plate, not saying a word.

"How is it?" I asked as Cameron shoveled food from his plate into his mouth.

"This cornbread is something else," he said, smiling at me.

"Well, I only make food for the best," I said jokingly before taking my plate to the other side of the table.

Somewhere among the cute conversations and flirtatious jokes that evening, I'd come to terms with the fact that I not only liked Cameron, but I wanted him. I couldn't keep it in for much longer.

That night when everyone left, Cameron stayed behind to help me straighten up a bit. We talked a little while cleaning up, and, as we tied the last trash bag up to sit in the trashcan on the curb, something inside of me urged me to come clean.

I walked him out of the house and, like loose teeth, it fell out of my mouth.

"I like you," I blurted without warning. I wanted to shove the words back into my mouth, but they had already been said.

I looked him in his deep, brown eyes that made me melt inside.

His eyebrows were raised, and his eyes were wide and showy. After a few seconds, he relaxed his face and began to smile awkwardly.

I didn't mean to say it, but my mouth fell wide open, and my confession fell right out.

"I—I mean, like, I used to have a crush on you. When we were little. Nothing serious." I stumbled over my words trying to crawl out of the hole I had just dug for myself.

"Oh, okay," he said with a sigh of relief. "That's really funny."

I shrugged my shoulders, still blushing with embarrassment, but relieved that he had taken my recant and ran with it.

I always wondered what would have happened if he knew I actually did like him.

A couple weeks went by, and nothing between Cameron and I had changed.

In November, I had my annual "Back to School Kickback." Everyone was going to be there. All of my friends from Tera Vista, Santiago, and Eastside.

I was known for throwing the most epic kickbacks—everyone always looked forward to attending one of my parties, and I thought nothing less of this one.

The party started getting live around ten o'clock. Cameron and Hunter arrived at around 10:30, and the party continued. We laughed. We drank. We danced to the music. It was a night that I knew I would never forget.

⁓

The upcoming week was Eastside's "Unity Week," or spirit week and, fortunately this year, I sat as the chair of the "Unity Week" festivities. It was a busy week for me. Between organizing the blood drive and making sure that all decorations for the dance had been delivered, I had no time for socializing in between events. So I forced my friends to come to the events in support.

Thursday was the blood drive, and the ASB team were to report to the school gym by 6:00 a.m. to ensure that all of the necessary equipment was set up. Throughout the week, Danielle, the student body president and a good friend of mine, was my right-hand girl. Danielle and I had become fast friends while working on council together. She was a great listener, and always gave sound advice, no matter the topic.

Thursday morning, Danielle and I found ourselves awaiting the kickoff of the blood drive. We had to be ready to accommodate half of the senior class and much of the junior class because it seemed as though everyone pledged to give blood that day.

When the bell rang, we walked to our assigned stations along with the other volunteers. Everyone was given a job, and I partook in each of them, but I spent most of my time in the hand-holder section. Volunteers in the hand-holder station had the job of comforting students while blood was being drawn. We would talk to them, make sure that they were at ease, and literally hold their hands if they needed it.

After about an hour, I changed stations. I was now at check-in, issuing liability waivers and consent forms to students who came to donate. I was happy with my responsibility until I noticed Cameron come into the gym from the opposite side of the double doors. Immediately, I began to devise a plan for how I would get to him.

I turned to the girl who was volunteering at the check-in station with me.

"I have to go back to the hand-holder station—it looks like they need help," I said, afraid that she would not believe my made-up excuse to change stations.

Volunteers had strict orders to stay at our designated stations throughout the duration of our shifts unless otherwise instructed to move.

The girl looked over my shoulder at the station, squinted her eyes, and gave me a shrug. I took it as her okaying me to leave, that she was fine manning the check-in station by herself. Quickly, I scurried across the floor to the station but, of course, someone was already stationed there. Luckily, the volunteer who just so happened to be there was Danielle.

"I need a huge favor," I said in the kindest tone.

"What's up?" she asked, still allowing the donor who she was serving to grip her hand.

"I need you to switch stations with me."

"Why?" she asked.

Without saying anything, I looked in Cameron's direction. He was sitting on the row of bleachers filling out forms.

"Oh, I get it," Danielle said with a sly smile. "Okay, after this guy," she said shaking the guy's hand, "we can switch."

I returned to the check-in table and continued with my designated duty until I got the cue form Danielle.

A few minutes passed, and I felt a tap on my shoulder. It was Danielle relieving me of my duty.

I peered around her to see the empty bed, but to my surprise, it wasn't empty anymore. Cameron was laying in it.

I looked up at Danielle from my chair with nervousness in my eyes. She chuckled and pulled on my arm to raise me up out of the chair.

As I walked up to Cameron's bed, he greeted me with his warm smile. I melted. His eye connected with mine, and I felt an instant connection.

I smiled back.

"Are you going to be a big baby?" I asked flirtatiously.

"If I am, will you hold my hand and wipe my tears?" He returned the flirtatious remark.

We talked for the thirty minutes it took for Cameron to get his blood drawn.

Every time we spoke, I fell for Cameron more and more and, by the end of this conversation, I knew that he was something I wanted.

As he finished up, I helped him up from the bed and walked him over to the recovery station.

"Thank you for staying with me," he said as I sat him down in a chair.

"You know I got you. Always will," I said with a slight smile.

I gave him his gift card for donating his blood.

I walked with him out of the gym just to make sure he didn't get faint on his way out.

"You know you owe me Starbucks for holding your hand in there," I said.

He smiled faintly. "I'll think about it," he said, giving me a nudge on the arm. "Text me what you want," he said, starting down the hall.

I stood there and watched him until he disappeared out of view, going out of the doors on the other side of the hall leading into the parking lot.

When I was sure that he wouldn't turn around, I scrambled to dig my phone out of my pocket. I found Cameron's name in my phone and went to my messages.

"Large strawberry water with four pumps of classic, please," I wrote, inserting a small red heart at the end.

As soon as I sent the text, Danielle appeared behind me.

"So Denise," she said with a smirk on her face, "you and Cam?"

I couldn't help but smile. I bit my bottom lip to keep my secret from falling from my mouth like confessions were known to do, but I couldn't hold on tight enough.

"Okay!" I blurted, "I like him, but I can't tell him. I'm just too scared. What if he doesn't like me back? What if he only sees me as a friend? What if—"

"Denise!" Danielle interrupted, "all of these 'what ifs,' but if you don't tell him, you'll never know."

And she was right. If I didn't tell him how I felt, I would never know if we could have possibly been something. Something more than friends.

"It's worth a shot," she said.

I nodded in agreement, and we both returned to the gym to begin wrapping up the stations for the blood drive.

While packing up the signs and posters, I felt my phone vibrate in my pocket. I slid my phone out of my pants and realized that Cameron had called me.

I moved my thumb across the screen and typed in my passcode to return his call.

"I'm back with your Starbucks," he said. "Come to the courtyard.

"Coming," I said and hung up my phone, making my way to the courtyard.

I met him in the courtyard. He gave me my drink and explained that he had been cleared to check out of school early that day, so he was going home.

He gave me a hug and walked out of the front gates.

I stayed in the courtyard for a few minutes, and my mind began to race.

I took out my phone and started typing:

I don't want this to come in between our friendship, and I don't want things to be awkward between me and you, but I do have to tell you something. I like you, Cameron, and I've liked you for a while now. I've always had a crush on you, and I just needed to get that out.

I pressed the send button and waited for a reply. Minutes felt like hours.

He finally wrote back:

Denise, nothing will ever ruin our friendship or make it awkward. If I'm being honest, I feel the same way. I hope that we stay close after high school. I mean, who knows? Maybe we can be something in the future. I really am happy to have you in my life though.

And there it was—the start of something new. This was the start of my second shot at love.

Friday was the last and most important day of "Unity Week."

Friday began with a morning rally in the courtyard before the second bell. After school was the dance.

Hunter had come with Ariel, his new girlfriend and one of my new friends and co-committee members for "Unity Week."

I climbed into Cameron's car, and I rode to school with him.

"I'm about to go smoke and pick up some breakfast—do you want anything?"

I was surprised. We weren't even together, but he was already volunteering to buy me food.

"You know I'm always hungry," I said, smiling. "I'll have what you have."

Even though it was just a fast food breakfast, his offer went a long way with me. Between that and falling asleep on FaceTime the night before, I felt as though we were taking steps in the direction of a relationship. We had a connection.

I slammed the door to his car and walked into the courtyard.

I carried the props over to the cheer team, who had been waiting at a table near the building entrance.

After a few minutes, the crackling of the intercom got everyone's attention. But this morning, instead of the morning announcements, music blared through the speakers.

All of a sudden, the cheerleaders flooded the middle of the courtyard and broke out in dance. Following the cheer team's performance were skits and a musical selection by the band.

The rally lasted about twenty minutes.

Cameron and Hunter made it back to campus just before the second bell rang. The second bell was referred to as the "tardy bell."

Cameron found me in the hallway and gave me the food he had ordered for me. I thanked him, gave him a hug, and we parted ways.

The pep rally got everyone excited, but we were all looking forward to the dance that night. I had spent so much time making sure that the decorations, the DJ, and everything else was in order for the dance, and I couldn't wait to see the turn out. I knew that it was bound to be a good night but, due to poor preparation on the part of the student council advisor and us not seeing eye to eye for some of the decisions that I had made on behalf of the dance committee, the dance was cancelled.

I had put so much time into making sure that spirit week was a success and half the students were either already there or were on their way. I was furious.

I stepped outside to get some fresh air. I called Cameron to vent. I knew he'd have something to say to lift my spirits.

"The dance is cancelled!"

"What?! Why? What happened?"

I hadn't heard his questions, but I answered them as if I had.

"Ms. Morrow never secured security for the dance, and now the administration is saying that we can't have it. How could they do this? I worked so hard for this! She told me not to come back to the council!"

I was furious.

"Calm down," he said. "You know, things happen. You did all that you could do, and the rest of the week was amazing!"

Somehow, Cameron always knew what to say to calm me down or make me feel better.

"How about this—since none of us have anything to do tonight, me and Hunter could just come over your place and have a movie night."

"That sounds like a plan," I said.

I hung up the phone and went back into the school to gather my things.

"Ariel!" I screamed across the gym, "I'm headed out. Hunter and Cam are coming over for movies. You down?"

She gave me a thumbs up and, with a nod, I left the gym and waited for her in the hallway.

Still angry, I didn't even wait around to see if the administration would change their decision. I simply told the rest of the committee that I was leaving, hopped in my car, and left. I agreed to drop some of the committee members off at their houses before heading home myself.

By the time I had dropped them off, Hunter and Cam were already on their way to my house.

When I got home, I told my mom what happened, that the dance had been cancelled, so Ariel, Hunter, and Cameron would be coming over to watch movies.

We ran upstairs and changed into sweats and sweat shirts to be a little more comfortable. When we heard the doorbell ring, we sprinted back down the stairs. I looked out the curtain to see Cameron's car sitting in front on my lawn. I opened the door and Hunter barged in.

"It's about time," he said, holding a bag full of snacks.

Cameron followed him in, and in his hand was a Starbucks cup.

"Here," he said handing the cup to me.

It was a strawberry water.

"I know you'd been having a bad day."

I blushed. "Thank you," I said, closing the door behind him.

We walked over to the living room, and I picked up the remote.

Ariel and Hunter made themselves comfortable on the loveseat, cuddling close together and draping the small throw blanket across both of their laps.

Cameron took a seat on the other couch. I went to turn off the lights. I returned to the living room to find that Cameron had taken the spot that I planned on sitting in.

"You're in my spot," I flirted.

"Oh, really?" Cameron replied.

"Yes, really."

"Well, I'm not moving," he said, smiling slyly.

Seeing that he was definite in his decision to stay where he was, I plopped down right beside him. He stretched out his arm, and I rested my head against it.

We had decided on watching Disney movies, but Hunter and Ariel didn't watch much of the movie. They were too busy sticking each other's tongues down one another's throats. Cameron and I didn't watch the movie either. We had become distracted by watching peoples' stories on Snapchat and having playful conversation.

Eventually, we put our phones down and continued watching the movie. I couldn't help but notice that Cameron had started to fall asleep. I pulled out my phone and took a picture of him. I posted it on my story on Snapchat and wrote the caption "sleepyhead" across it.

By midnight, we had all been either sleep or dozing off. I

stopped the movie, and we all got up. Hunter and Ariel left. Ariel had volunteered to take Hunter home.

I walked Cameron outside to his car, and we gave one another a hug before he left. The hug was long and warm. It was meaningful. I could feel his heart beating and, with his arms wrapped around me, I felt secure. I was melting inside, and butterflies flew through my stomach. He let go, and a part of me felt sad, never wanting the hug to end. He unlocked his car door, and walked to the other side.

"Text me as soon as you get home," I ordered.

I needed to know that he got home safely.

He started his engine, and I returned to my doorstep.

When he drove off, I walked back inside.

I was on cloud nine. I hadn't felt this feeling in a while, and I certainly didn't think that this feeling was going to come from someone whom I'd known almost my entire life.

I ran upstairs, turned off my bedroom light, and laid in my bed waiting for his text. My mind began to wander. I thought about the night, and how I had fallen for Cameron even more.

My thoughts were interrupted by the bright light on my phone screen and a loud vibrating noise. I reached for my phone on my dresser and, just as I had expected, it was Cameron.

I'm home. I really enjoyed spending the night with you, he wrote.

I was beaming. By this time, I was head over heels.

Thanks for coming, and thanks for the Starbucks. Oh, and go check my last post on Snapchat, I replied.

It took him a minute to respond.

Don't worry. I'm going to get you back, he wrote.

I had directed him to the picture of him sleeping earlier that night.

I'd like to see you try.

I responded and, even though I didn't want to, I wished him a goodnight and drifted off to sleep.

CHAPTER SEVEN

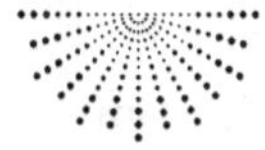

*Love: a warm, cherished feeling that gives you hope and lightens up
the soul*

The Saturday following "Unity Week" marked the beginning of preseason for Eastside basketball. Luckily, cheerleaders weren't required to cheer at preseason games, so I got to go with my friends instead of with the team.

The first game of preseason was an away game at Canal High in Corona, and Briana, Ariel, and I had made plans to go together.

Cameron was going to be there too. We were all going to support Hunter.

These games weren't formal affairs—I usually threw on a school T-shirt and some jeans—but, for some reason, I was stressing out about what I was going to wear to this particular game. After the night I had with Cam, I had to make sure I looked my best when he saw me. I wanted to catch his eye. I wanted him to do a double take when he saw me.

That night I decided on wearing some distressed jeans with an oversized sweater shirt and a pair of Jordans. I curled my hair, did my makeup, and waited for Briana to pick me up.

We pulled up to the high school and walked into the gym. We scanned the bleachers for people we knew and spotted our friends in the crowd. So we made our way over to them. As we walked past the crowd of spectators, Cameron caught my eye sitting among the group. We pushed through the seated fans and sat in front of our group of friends.

"Hey, everyone!" I said, trying to make room for three.

"Do you mind if I rest my back on your legs?" I asked Cameron, attempting to get comfortable on the hard, wooden bleachers.

"Yes, I mind," he said jokingly.

I shoved his legs and turned straight in the bleacher, using Cameron's legs as support.

The game was intense, and the boys were playing hard. Briana, Ariel, and I cheered at the top of our lungs, especially when Hunter got in the game. Even though the boys didn't win, they played one hell of a game that night.

Just like every other game, we always went to Denny's following the game.

"Are you coming?" I asked Cameron as everyone filed out of the gym.

"I'll meet you guys up there after I pick up my car," he assured me.

We arrived at Denny's and, as usual, Briana and I ordered more food than we could eat, and Ariel didn't order anything, knowing that our leftovers would be just enough for her to eat as well.

What was supposed to be an outing among friends turned into a girls' night until Hunter walked through the doors.

"What's up, y'all?!" Hunter asked, walking over to our table and pushing Ariel to the inside of the booth with his body. He ordered his food, and we all waited for him to finish eating before deciding to go back to my house to hang out.

Hey! Hunter, Briana, and Ariel are all coming over tonight you in? I texted Cameron.

No doubt. I'll meet you there, he replied.

We paid for our tabs and left, me riding with Briana, and Ariel riding with Hunter.

~

The night consisted of us watching movies, cuddling with one another, and engaging in playful conversation.

At around midnight, Hunter decided that it was time to go home, so he and Ariel gathered their things and left. Briana had left much earlier. I think she felt like a third wheel among a couple of couples. Cameron, however, stayed behind.

I turned on Cameron's favorite movie, and we watched until we began to doze off. I woke up to his arm wrapped around my shoulder.

"Wake up," I whispered. "I'm about to go up to my room."

He stirred a little but didn't wake.

"Cameron?" I shook him softly.

His eyes opened, and he looked around the living room.

"Whoa," he said, rubbing his eyes with his palms, "I guess it's time for me to go."

I leaned away from him, giving him enough room to stand up from the couch.

He got up and started to put on his shoes.

I watched him as he moved lazily across the room to gather his things.

I guess he felt my eyes following his every movement because after a few minutes he looked up at me.

"What you looking at?" he said playfully.

I shook my head and smiled.

"Come here, I have to tell you a secret," I said as he pulled his sweatshirt over his head.

He walked over to the couch and leaned in close to me to receive the secret I had promised him. Just when he got close enough, I moved toward his face and our lips locked.

Butterflies shot around in my stomach. I felt so much passion in the kiss, and I knew it was right. It was beautiful and, as he pulled away, we both had big cheesy smiles spread across our faces.

"Alright, get out my house," I told him, still smiling from ear-to-ear.

"Well, that's rude," he laughed.

I walked him outside and, as we walked toward the curb toward his car, he stopped me right before the driveway, pulled me by my waist into his body and, standing face to face, *he* kissed *me*.

I looked in his eye, and I felt him look deep into my soul.

At that moment, I felt like the luckiest girl in the world. The butterflies that had finally settled down after the first kiss felt as though they had exploded in my stomach.

As we released again, our eyes connected, and I knew in that very moment that I was in love… again.

When you first fall in love, you are not too sure what love is. I called my first love the love of my life because he was my first experience, my first rodeo. I was new to the experience of dating and new to the idea of relationships. I was not sure of what to expect from it, and I was not sure of what it was supposed to feel like or how it all worked.

But, in this moment, at that very second, I knew *this* was something different, and I knew that Cameron was someone special.

On Sunday, Cameron came over for our weekly study day. Ariel and Hunter also came. That day, Cameron and I let the world know we were together.

We had been studying for about an hour, or pretended to study as we joked around. I finally worked up the nerve to tell Ariel and Hunter what I had been wanting to tell them all day.

"So, Cameron and I have decided to get together," I said hesitantly, waiting for Ariel and Hunter's reaction.

They both looked at me with wide eyes, Ariel smiling, Hunter seemingly skeptical.

"You're lying," he said.

"We have no reason to lie," Cameron interjected.

"Prove it," Hunter demanded.

I took out my phone and held the phone up to take a picture of me and Cameron together as we kissed. I snapped the picture and posted it on Twitter.

"See?"

I turned the phone to Hunter to show him the picture I had posted. I made sure that Hunter, Ariel, and the rest of the world know that Cameron and I were a thing.

Immediately after posting the photo, my phone beeped. It was a text message from Bryant. He wasn't too happy about the photo, but I didn't care. It was my decision and no one else's.

We were not in an official relationship just yet, but we were working toward a relationship, working towards something more serious than what we already had. I was falling for him, and I was falling hard, so hard I couldn't stop myself.

"Cameron?"

"What's up?"

"I love you," I said one night as we talked on the phone, "but it's okay if you don't love me back."

Just like with Bryant, I had gotten attached rather quickly and, even before confessing my love, I already knew that Cameron wasn't in love with me, but I knew there was a strong possibility that one day he would be.

And I was okay with that.

~

The first week of us "talking," Cameron asked me out on our first date.

He took me on my *real* first date. When he came to pick me up, he made sure that he met with my parents. Even though he already knew them, his gesture showed me that we were playing a completely different game than the one I was used to.

He picked me up from my house. I had no idea where we were going but, after begging him to tell me, he finally caved.

He was taking me to the Cheesecake Factory.

"You know, I actually hate the Cheesecake Factory," I said with a smirk.

Days before, he had asked Briana for suggestions regarding where he should take me and, of all places, she said Cheesecake Factory.

"Really? I actually don't like it that much either, I just thought you'd like it," he said laughing. "How about we just go to Buffalo Wild Wings?"

As Cam maneuvered the car to make a U-turn and head the opposite direction, BAM! Everything took a turn for the worse. Another car came crashing into the passenger side of Cameron's car.

My body jerked side to side, and my head hit the radio.

The car was damaged, but the important thing was that everyone was okay.

"Are you okay?!" Cameron asked frantically. "Denise, are you okay?"

"I'm fine," I said, trying to refocus my vision and keep my composure.

Cameron hopped out of the car to assess the damage, and see if the passengers in the other vehicle were okay.

He came back to the car and poked his head in. "Call Hunter to come pick you up, I have to handle this."

I called Hunter, and he came in fifteen minutes.

I watched Cameron from Hunter's car as he talked to Hunter,

and I could see him shaking. Tears had begun to flow down his face.

I got out of the car and walked over to them.

"Are you going to be okay?" I asked, trying to calm him down.

He looked at me, pulled me close to his body, and hugged me tight.

"I'm just glad you're okay," he whispered. "I don't know what I would have done if I lost you," he said before I left. Tears continued to flow down his cheeks.

Of all of the things he could have worried about, the thing that he seemed to be most relieved about was me being okay. This was the moment that I realized that I meant a lot to him. In his eyes, I saw the love that he had for me and, though he didn't say it, it was in that moment that I realized that he loved me.

When I got into Hunter's car, I broke down in tears. I was scared. Both of our lives could have ended that easily.

Hunter took me home, and I told my parents about what had happened.

"Are you okay?" my dad asked. "How'd it happen?"

I stumbled over my tongue to explain all of the details of the accident.

Hunter had come inside and waited for me to get my keys. We had decided we would both go check on Cameron.

About an hour later, Hunter drove us over to Cameron's to see how he was.

"How are you?" Hunter asked as we sat in Cameron's living room.

"I think I'm fine, now," Cameron said. He looked tired, and his shoulders drooped.

"Hey, I know what will make you feel better," Hunter said, smiling. "We can go grab a bite to eat at Denny's."

Cameron immediately perked up. "On you?" he asked.

We all laughed. "Sure," Hunter said.

We all piled in Hunter's car and made our way to Denny's, where we dined in.

On the way home, we laughed and talked—we even picked up Ariel.

Even with all of the night's events, it ended on a good note.

After we all finished eating, Hunter took everyone home, dropping off Cam first, then me, then Ariel.

As we approached my house, Hunter stopped the car and waited on me to get out.

As I was getting out the car my phone vibrated. It was Cam.

I had stopped in the middle of the street to give the messages my undivided attention.

The text sent a surge through my body.

My eyes lit up as I read the screen, and a smile spread across my face. It was a smile so bright that it could have outshined the streetlights that hovered above my head.

I had found it. I found love once again, but this time I knew it was the real love. The love that gets you tied up and overwhelmed. The love that pushes you to the limit, tests your patience, and changes you. The love that takes over your entire world and completes your puzzle.

I read the text one more time and replied with the same response.

I walked into my house and crept up to my room, the message still on my mind. That night, I fell asleep with the image of the text etched into my brain.

I love you, it read.

~

Cameron and I made it official December 21, 2014. Our relationship was very different from anything I had ever experienced. He was my other half. He was my everything. There was nothing I wouldn't do for this man. We took on the remainder of senior year together, and he became my biggest support system.

He was not only my boyfriend, but he was also my best friend. He was my "Mexican Crush Monday," and I was his "Weave Crush Wednesday."

There was something about Cam that made him different from other guys, something that made me fall completely in love with him.

Cameron was Cameron and nothing could ever change that. He was caring. He was supportive. He was encouraging. He inspired me to push towards my dreams and accomplish my goals. He was an uplifting spirit, my blessing from the Lord.

He was something I never thought of losing. Of course, like any other relationship, we had our honeymoon stage, but ours seemed as if would last forever. We were genuinely happy with one another, and nothing could affect that. I only had eyes for him, and I knew he felt the same way about me.

Before Cam and I made it official, I had to give him my "spill."

"You know I've been hurt before, Cameron. I don't want to be hurt again," I told him *any* chance I got.

"I know, Denise. I'm not going to hurt you," he'd always say before giving me a light kiss on my forehead.

He promised me that he'd try the best he could to do right by me, and that even at his worst, he'd never do to me what Bryant had done to me.

I believed him and jumped head first into the relationship.

That same year, we spent our first Christmas together.

That year for Christmas I made him a "Dating Denise" survival kit. The box was decorated in Christmas wrapping paper, and I filled it with small gifts. It had letters filled with words of encouragement and love. I put a sweater in it because I stole all of his sweaters when we were together. I also threw in a tube of lip balm in there because he would always use mine and some mittens because his hands were always cold.

I told him that the box would get him through our relationship.

He introduced me to all of his family, and they soon started to feel just like my family. Although I worried about our relationship because of our ethnicities—I was black, and he was Hispanic—both my family and his family accepted us with open arms.

CHAPTER EIGHT

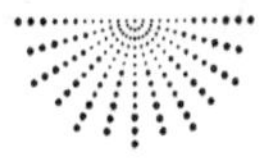

*Love: an everlasting feeling; to feel complete and whole with the
company of someone you call your own*

By Valentine's Day 2015, I was ready to give Cameron the world. I
had been planning his Valentine's Day gift for months, and I knew
that it had to be something special. I saved for two months and
worked my butt off to give him something that would show
exactly how much I loved him.

I was the creative type of girlfriend. Every gift I gave
Cameron had tons of love and a lot of time and thought put
into it. I paid close attention to the things he said he liked and
made sure they were all interpreted in his Valentine's Day gift.
The first part of the gift was huge and involved a lot of work
and help. I had convinced his mother to get him out of the
house early that morning, and I went over to his house and
decorated his entire room with twelve red heart balloons scat-
tered about the room. At the end of each string was a notecard.
Written on the notecard was an intimate message. I posted
pictures all over his walls of nearly every photo we had
together, and on the back of the photo was a small message that

described the moment captured. Finally, I left a tray of red velvet cupcakes on his desk along with chocolate-covered strawberries.

I wrote up a letter and placed it in the center of his bed.

Dinner at 6? Meet me at Briana's, the letter read.

I hadn't texted Cam that entire day to make sure that his Valentine's Day gift would be a surprise. This Valentine's Day, Briana, Ariel, and I all had boyfriends, so we all decided to celebrate Valentine's as couples.

That night Cameron looked at me like he had never looked at me before. He looked at me like I was the lady of his life. I felt like this could last for an eternity. I knew that one day I would say "I do," to this man, and I was perfectly content with being his girl for the rest of my life.

After dinner, we drove to the top of the Siesta, a mountain a few miles outside of the city. We reached the top of the mountain and just sat in our cars staring down at the city lights, enjoying the view.

I had one more gift for Cameron, a gift that could not be bought nor replaced. It was a gift that I was saving for my potential lifetime partner. I was in love with Cameron, and I saw our relationship as a lifetime thing. I believed that I was going to spend the rest of my life with him.

We sat in his car making light conversation.

"I'm glad that I got to spend this Valentine's with you," he said.

"Me too," I returned.

Love was definitely in the air and, as Cameron leaned in to kiss me, I could fill my heart leap as if jumping toward his.

At first, only our lips touched until he reached for me, cupping his hand around my neck then slowly moving it to my shoulder, then all the way down to my waist.

My body tingled and my hands got clammy, but I liked it.

He stopped kissing and leaned away just far enough away from my lips to speak.

"You know? We don't have to do this if you don't want to," he said, hand still resting on my waist.

"Don't stop," I whispered back, "I want you to have me."

We continued.

By now, there was not one part of my body that Cameron's hands hadn't explored.

I leaned back in the seat and slipped my arms from under the straps of my romper, and Cameron followed me, pressing me against the passenger door.

His lips went from my lips, to my neck, to my shoulders.

When he got to my chest, he stopped.

"Are you sure?" he asked. "We don't have to do this if you're not ready."

I slipped down my black lace panties and allowed Cameron to have every part of me.

He was my first, and I thought that the he would be my last. That the person I gave my virginity to would one day be my husband and the father of my children.

It's crazy how you believe in all this at such a young age. I was so caught up in this man, and he was all tied up in me. We saw a future with each other, and I figured this would be the last person I would tell the words "I love you" to.

Our relationship didn't end there. We dated throughout our senior year and graduated together and, though we had different dream schools—I wanted to attend San Jose State and he wanted to go to Baylor—we settled on Cal Polytechnic so that we could be close to home and, more importantly, so that we could be together.

He gave me a raw unconditional love, and I thanked the Lord every day for blessing me with this unique individual. We centered our relationship around the important things; together we built a relationship with the Lord, supported each other through our senior year, and set goals for each other that we planned on accomplishing together. We got accepted to the same college, and we graduated together, both receiving academic honor roll.

We had it all planned, but we never planned for the problems that would come along trying to balance college and a relationship.

Our problems were small, but I began to realize that his smoking had turned from recreational to a habit. I knew Cameron smoked, and I didn't have a problem with it at first, but it seemed as if it was becoming an addiction.

"Can you even go a day without smoking?" I asked him one night as we sat in his room supposed to be studying.

"What are you talking about?" he asked, opening a pack of milds.

I watched him as he dumped the tobacco from the milds to replace it with marijuana.

And that's where it started. That is the moment I began trying to change Cameron. I noticed myself trying to take control of not only his habit, but everything that he did, thinking it was for the better.

I hope you're in your room studying and not at some party, I'd text him.

I simply wanted him to be the best version of himself that he could be.

Our relationship was perfect, and I found joy in taking control and fighting and bickering with Cameron just to get my way. I was testing him. I wanted to see if he would leave me. I wanted to see if he would leave his bad habits.

After a while, Cameron expressed how he was tired of our constant bickering and my controlling attitude so, like any reasonable person would, he left my house.

The next day, I surprised Cameron by coming over to his house without notice. We had gotten into an argument earlier that week because of a lie that he had told me. Rather than admitting that he was using most of his free time to smoke, he convinced me that he was putting in extra hours of studying for a test, or that he was doing homework that was starting to pile up.

Cameron didn't like to disappoint me, so the alternative to that was lying to me. Little did he know, I hated being lied to more than I hated being disappointed.

Once he lied to me about his smoking, I found it hard to believe him with other things. Even with the smallest matters, I swore he was lying to me. I no longer trusted him and, because of that, trust issues began to control me in regards to how I treated Cameron.

Cameron opened the door, and I immediately went in for a hug. I just wanted to feel his embrace, but I was quickly disappointed when I inhaled and my lungs filled with the scent of smoke. He leaned in and kissed me, and I could taste marijuana on his breath.

"Have you been smoking?" I asked.

Moments like these turned small issues into major situations. One question turned into full-blown arguments.

Back and forth, but nothing ever got solved.

I was sure Cameron would one day decide that he was tired of me arguing and my control and that he would call it quits, but I carried on.

"Look, Cameron, it's either me or weed," I said.

I had to give him an ultimatum, and I had no doubt that he would choose me.

I was wrong.

I left Cameron's but, after reflecting on the situation the whole ride home, I had to come to terms with the fact that it was not his fault. I knew that Cameron smoked when he asked me out, but my stubbornness to accept what I couldn't change, and my controlling attitude did nothing but magnify the situation. I picked fights about small things, I tried to change him, and I simply could not accept the fact that he wasn't perfect, but who was?

After thinking long and hard, I called Cameron to tell him that the ultimatum was off the table, and that his habit would not push me away when his love drew me so close.

CHAPTER NINE

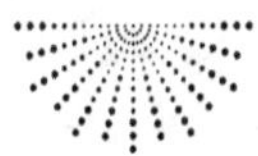

Love: a force that attracts you, emotionally and physically

November 3rd. The day I was brought into this world. Birthdays are supposed to be joyous days filled with laughter, love, and well wishes—the one day of the year meant for you to feel special.

My birthday had always been a big deal. But this year, I felt like it would be different. I had an amazing boyfriend and, even though we were not on perfect terms, I knew he would make my birthday something to remember, and that he did.

Every year I planned outings for me, my close friends, and family.

It was my eighteenth birthday and, like every year, Briana came over the night before to spend the night with me and be with me to bring in my birthday. Briana always wanted to be the first one to wish me a happy birthday, but this year, I wanted Cameron to be the one to bring in my birthday with me.

Midnight came and went, and I had not gotten a text from Cameron.

I woke to my vibrating phone.

Get up and come outside, my friend Aydian had texted.

I rolled out of bed and slid on a pair of sweat pants. I walked downstairs and went to the front door to find Aydian standing on my front porch with cards and candy.

Aydian was a special case. Although our relationship was strictly platonic, he was a good friend and was always there for me in the moments I felt like Cameron wasn't.

Cameron did *not* like Aydian, but I never felt like he had any reason not to.

"I don't trust him around you," Cameron would say.

Even though he said he didn't trust Aydian, I always had it in the back of my mind that it was *me* he didn't trust.

Cameron had a million girl friends, and I never hassled him about that.

"You have friends who are girls, and I respect that. I just would like to have the same respect," I'd argue.

We argued a lot about Aydian, but Aydian wasn't the problem. The problem was the double standard. Aydian was just one of many examples of how double standards dictated our relationship.

Cameron could have girl friends, but I couldn't have guy friends.

Cameron could drink, I couldn't.

Everything that Cameron could do was unacceptable when I did it.

And this was the beginning of our end.

Aydian bought me a card and some candy for my birthday, I texted Cameron.

For what? I hope you gave it back, he replied.

I didn't.

What the hell, Denise?! You know how I feel about that.

Well, at least he was up at midnight to be there to wish me a happy birthday!

I sat up in the bed to get closer to eye level. I was fuming. Not because he was asleep, but because he should have been the one to call me, not Aydian. Deep down, I just wanted those first moments to be spent with the person I loved. Even though Cam did help me celebrate my birthday, I wanted more, and in my stubbornness, I pushed away the efforts that he did make.

For my birthday, Cameron had gotten me flowers, candy, and a large Victoria's Secret bag and box with shoes that he left on my front porch. It was no way to deliver a gift, and it pissed me right off. I took it as Cameron not wanting to spend time with me. Later, I learned that he had car and work troubles, but I didn't forgive him. In my mind, he should have tried harder to make sure that he was there.

I confronted Cameron about his absence, and I said some things that I shouldn't have said.

Cameron came over around seven that night; my dad was making my favorite birthday meal, so my mom sent me and Cameron to the store to get my birthday cake. I had a damn attitude; I wanted nothing to do with him because it took him all day to even show up at my house.

We sat in the parking lot and he asked me what my problem was.

At first I replied and said, "Nothing," but nothing turned into to something really fast.

"You haven't been with me all day. I don't even feel like you care, and you just ruined my birthday after I told you how much it meant to me to actually try and have a good birthday for one year."

I don't remember all of the nasty, degrading things that I called him, but I'm sure I know what tipped the scale.

"You're no better than Bryant!" I remember saying, and that was the last thing I said in the argument.

He called me ungrateful and cursed me the fuck out.

After everything died down and we said our apologies, we kissed and made up, but deep down inside I was still hurt. I felt like he didn't care.

~

My behaviors were just like the behaviors that hurt me. Cameron had shown me nothing but love, and I rejected it.

I was degrading. I was cruel, and I said things to him I would never want spoken to me. I turned into a bottle of yellow paint and instead of me eating it, I was forcing Cameron to, but Cam was not like me—he did not sit there with an open mouth.

That's the thing: when you get hurt, you never really get over it. The pain never really goes away, and you never forget how that one person made you feel. Somehow you just learn to deal with it, or you turn into it.

I had to come to my senses that this man didn't deserve what I gave him. He was the only man that I knew who loved me despite my flaws, and despite my insecurities. Even though I didn't deserve any part of him, I was extremely grateful that he always stayed.

On Saturday, I had a birthday dinner, and afterward, my friends and I decided to go to a nightclub being that I was the last one to turn eighteen.

I had plans to get my makeup done, and I had bought a sexy, navy blue suede dress with nude suede pumps to match. I did my hair in loose waves, and I was ready to slay.

My dinner consisted of all my close friends and a few of my childhood friends and, of course, the love of my life. I could feel the love that surrounded me.

The night was perfect, and Cameron wanted to make sure that I got the most out of my birthday weekend.

"We should go to L.A.," he told me. He wanted to take me out there as his way of making up for what had happened on my birthday.

"When?!" I asked excitedly.

"Tonight."

My smile immediately turned.

We all had planned to go out, but it had gotten late so my parents said that I couldn't go.

"I can't," I said, but Cameron didn't care.

"We're just going to go to the club," he said, and that pissed me right off.

"Why the hell do you need to go to the club with them?! Am I ruining your fun on *my* birthday? That makes no sense!"

It was a never-ending argument with Cameron, and I was always in the wrong. I couldn't understand how he could think what he was doing was okay. Once again, I would be left spending my birthday with people I loved but not him. All I wanted was him, and I felt like at every chance he got, he drifted further and further away from me. Our relationship was slowly falling through the cracks of my fingers and, no matter how I tried to gather all the pieces, it was becoming impossible to catch them all. Day after day, the problems seemed to continue to pile on top of one another.

When we left the restaurant that night, Cameron went one way, and I went another, which further added to my discontent.

I woke up still thinking of the argument Cameron and I had the previous night, and now I regretted inviting him and his mother to my birthday brunch. We played nice in front of both of our families.

When it came to Cam, I put on a façade to cover up our real problems because I felt that it was no one's business what was going on between us. Besides, I usually knew that we would be able to work it out.

But this time, the problems that we were having seemed impossible to fix.

Brunch was going great, but I noticed that Cameron had mentally removed himself from the group. He was quiet and, for a majority of the time, he had his nose in his phone.

I looked around the table until I caught the eye of Alexandra, my cousin. Alexandra was sitting right next to Cameron, and I was at the head of the table.

She looked up at me. "Switch places with me," I mouthed to her discreetly, hoping that no one saw my gesture.

She squinted her eyes. "What?" she mouthed back.

"I have to talk to Cameron. Let's switch," I added in hand gestures to help her get the point.

"Oh," she said, nodding her head, pushing away from the table, and walking toward the head of the table.

I got up from my seat and settled in the seat next to Cameron. I looked at him, nose still buried in his phone, but he didn't notice. I rested my head on his shoulder and snuggled against him, hoping to get his attention. He stopped texting and looked at me.

I glanced at his phone, though my intentions weren't to be nosey, and immediately I noticed the name on his phone.

Rebecca.

It was one of his female co-workers and, from the looks of it, the conversation didn't seem to be work-related. The messages were riddled with emojis.

Flirtatious emojis.

I drew back, not wanting to see something that I might not have liked. I didn't want to see it, and I didn't want to believe it if I did see it.

"Why are you texting her?" I asked, whispering so as to not draw attention to the conversation.

"She needs to switch shifts with me," he explained.

I half-heartedly believed what he told me, and I left it at that. I didn't want to make a big scene. Not at my brunch. It was not the time nor the place for an argument.

~

By Monday, the thought of Cameron texting Rebecca still sat in my head.

Alexandra and I attended the same college. She was one year older than me. Alexandra was my gift from the Lord. I looked up to her and, over the course of the year, we had become extremely close. She was the one who I would always run to for advice about Cameron because she was also in a long-term relationship.

I looked up to Alexandra and trusted her guidance. She was smart and kind, and her personality fit with mine like a puzzle piece.

My boyfriend and Alexandra's boyfriend were a lot alike, so she would know exactly what needed to be done when I came to her about any problems that I was having with Cameron.

What should I do about the text messages? I texted Alexandra before my second class.

She told me to ask for screenshots of the messages.

After prodding for what seemed like hours, Cameron finally broke and sent me screenshots of the entire conversation he had had with Rebecca.

I read through the messages, and I could tell that some had been deleted. There were time gaps and some of the responses didn't align with the messages that were supposedly sent moments prior.

"Here we go again," I thought.

Rebecca had become the center of our relationship and the source of my insecurities.

It turned out that Cameron and Rebecca were very well acquainted with one another. I found out that they regularly hung out together outside of work, they smoked together, and to top it all off, Cameron had been going to her for help with his "relation-ship problems."

But according to Cameron, they were "just friends."

As a girl, when we hear these words, we see red. I went absolutely crazy.

This girl was working her way into Cameron's heart. In my eyes, she had zero boundaries and zero respect for my relationship. She knew who I was because I always visited Cameron at work and he always introduced me as his girlfriend.

I tried not to assume anything about Rebecca's motives, but Cameron confided in this girl, and I had no respect for it. It was a complete slap in the face. He had lied to me about their relationship, and he was going behind my back to spend time with her; even if it was just smoking, they were still sharing a connection with one another. Rebecca had officially become a threat to our relationship.

I was furious. It was an obvious case of the double standard because if I were to have a male friend like Rebecca was to Cameron, I would have for sure been a single girl. He would have broken up with me, no questions asked.

In that moment, I knew I was going to lose Cameron to Rebecca. In that moment, I knew she was going to be his next lover. In that moment, I knew our relationship was crashing before my eyes and, even though I tried everything in my power to stop its plight, I also did everything in my power to push Cameron away.

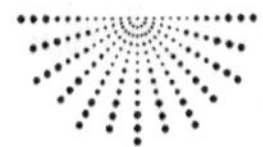

CHAPTER TEN

Love: a feeling that is built up to break you down

Our one-year anniversary came, and it was the worst first-year anniversary that I could have ever imagined.

Cameron and I initially planned to go to Disneyland and spend the whole day together but, due to the holidays being so soon and Cam not planning far enough in advance, he couldn't take off from work.

The night before our anniversary, Cameron had decided to go out with his friends and smoke instead of spending time with me, knowing that he would be working on our actual anniversary.

I, on the other hand, sat at home with Lisa, one of my teammates.

"Can you believe Cameron?" I fumed, pacing around my room in frustration, "It's our anniversary and he decides to go smoke instead of spend time with me."

"Yeah, that's mad crazy," Lisa agreed, flipping through pages of a magazine. "So what are you going to do?" she asked.

I stopped pacing and looked at Lisa. What was I going to do?

I figured it was now time to show Cameron exactly how he

made me feel. I told myself I would never let another man take advantage of me. I promised myself I would never let another person hurt me again. So I called Aydian.

"Hey, Aydian," I said as soon as the phone stopped ringing through the receiver.

"What's up, D?" Aydian responded.

"Well, I want to try something," I said. I could feel my hands getting clammy. "I want to come smoke with you."

"Seriously?!" Aydian said, laughing into the receiver.

"Why?! I mean, I'm down, but this is not like you."

He was right. This wasn't like me, but I wanted to show Cameron that just like he could smoke with his girl friends on *our* anniversary, I could smoke with my guy friends.

Later that evening, I admitted to Cameron that I had gone to smoke with Aydian. He was infuriated.

"What the hell, Denise?!" he screamed through the phone. "Why would you do that?!" Every foul word he could think of, he called me.

At first I was happy that he could finally experience the anger that I had when he went to smoke with Rebecca, but soon I realized that revenge was not the way to settle the issue. I felt a deep regret for what I had done, but by then, the damage was done.

So, I tried to cover it up.

"It wasn't just Aydian there, it was a group of us. I didn't know Aydian would be there."

Half of what I said was the truth, and the other half was a lie.

"I didn't do it to get back at you," I said, but in my heart, I knew that that was exactly what I did.

I was fighting fire with fire, and I soon had to realize that even though Cameron was getting burned, I was getting burned too.

～

I had lied to Cameron about my intentions when I smoked with Aydian, but soon enough, the truth came out.

It was New Year's Eve, and my entire family went out of town for the holiday. I couldn't go because I had work, so I stayed home and planned on spending my New Year's Eve with Cameron. It was our second New Year's as a couple.

We were going to watch movies and just stay in and be with each other the whole night.

Halfway into the night, I went to shower just in case I fell asleep later. I went upstairs and, when I came back down, Cameron was gone.

My heart dropped as I peered around the couch and noticed my phone sitting face up, unlocked. I looked at the screen and the messages between me and Aydian were open.

Immediately, I called Cameron. No answer.

I called and called. No answer.

I texted him and called until he answered.

"Cameron, can we talk about this?" I pleaded.

Reluctantly, he agreed to come back to my house, but it wasn't to let me explain.

I got on my knees, and I begged for him. I cried, but he wasn't trying to hear it. I cried what seemed to be an endless stream of tears.

What had I done? Why did I do this? I allowed the one thing that mattered to me to slip away. I took away my happiness. I broke my own heart.

In my eyes, he had no real reason to be upset. I did exactly what he had done to me, but he couldn't take it. He didn't like it, and unlike me, he wasn't so forgiving.

We brought in the new year arguing.

He lay next to me and watched me cry. I was a mess. I wanted him to just let it go like I eventually did. I wanted him to see that it was a stupid mistake and that I realized my mistake.

But this was his ticket out, and he took it and ran with it.

I woke up the next morning, and it all felt unreal. I didn't think we were done. I thought it was just a little bump in the road, but it wasn't.

I was sick that day, and I didn't want to do much. I really had no strength to be anything other than miserable.

I messed up something that meant so much to me. All I wanted was him. I wasn't just losing my boyfriend. I was losing half of my heart. The person that meant the absolute world to me, the person I thought would one day get my "I do." I was jealous and insecure and just *had* to be the one to get even.

I tried to drive down to Glamis that day to be with my family, but I couldn't even bring myself to go because I couldn't stop crying.

I slept for most of the day and well into the night.

I woke up to my phone buzzing underneath my pillow at three o'clock in the morning. I was half asleep when I answered the phone.

"Denise?" my mother said. Her voice was light and raspy. "I have some bad news."

"What is it?" I asked, sitting up in my bed.

"Caden passed away in the hospital last night. It was about two hours ago."

I couldn't believe what I was hearing. Caden was my cousin. I had confided in him many times about Cameron and he had all the right answers on how to fix our relationship. Just a week ago, Caden and Cameron had met at Christmas dinner for the first time.

I had no feeling left inside of me—it was like my soul left my body, and I was just a walking zombie. I did not know how to react or take it in for that matter. I did not believe it, not for one second.

"Don't mess this up, cousin. You know have a keeper," he would joke.

I rushed over to Caden's family's house and, as soon as I

entered, I could feel the pain and grief in the room. This was real. Caden was really gone. He wasn't just any person. Caden had soul that brightened the room. He was funny and goofy, kindhearted and loving. He was a brother to me.

I stayed for a few hours, then drove back home

As I drove home, I broke down. He was gone. I would never get to share another memory with him. I was all alone—no family, no one to comfort me. I felt cold inside. I ended up calling Cameron; I needed him more than ever at this moment. My mom and dad were too far, and I couldn't get through this alone. I went crazy. I was unstable; I had never dealt with a pain like this before. I felt as if everything bad was just happening to me, and I did not know how to cope with it

The funeral was hard. I felt my weakest that day, but what was even harder was the fact that Cam stuck around but had no intentions of getting back with me. He only stayed to comfort me while I grieved.

I wanted to rip the Band-Aid off all at once, to get over the pain of losing my cousin and losing the one I loved.

But it didn't happen that way.

I didn't know how to cope with the loss of two people I loved. I was willing to do anything just to spend time with Cameron. It was a loss I wasn't willing to have. I couldn't imagine myself with someone else, and I wanted him back.

I felt cold and powerless to accept everything that was going wrong. My heart just needed a break. I wanted to feel something again. I was dealing with too much and, once again, my depression revisited me.

I lost interest in school. I lost interest in God. I lost interest in life altogether.

My happiness was non-existent.

I was throwing my body to Cameron, hoping he would consider getting back together with me. I was failing my classes and barely going to work.

I was, once again, in a dark place, unsure of how I was going to get through this time.

I just wanted my life back and, at this point, I felt like everything was just getting taken away from me.

Cameron and I were still dealing with each other and, even though I felt like we were getting back together, he was clearly just looking for sex and someone to talk to at his convenience. Cameron didn't want to be with me, and I couldn't accept that fact.

∼

Months went by and things started to get easier. I was getting better, day by day.

It was getting closer to summer, and I was still pushing to try to work things out with Cameron. I couldn't give up on him, and I didn't want to. I was so emotionally invested in him and his family, and I wasn't going to, but he beat the fight right out of me.

I loved Cameron, and I just wanted to see him happy.

I could tell he had started talking to another girl. I would stalk his Twitter, look through his "Favorites," and see the conversations he was having. Most of the conversations were with the same girl.

I would look through his "Favorites," and I would follow the threads of conversation that he would have. When we rode to school together, I would go through his phone and constantly argue and cry to express to him how much I needed him and wanted him back in my life.

But I soon began to get tired of it all.

I knew I could no longer make him happy. This girl was becoming a factor in his life. So I tried to push him away.

"If you like her, go be with her," I would tell him. "If she makes you happy, go. We can just be friends."

I wanted Cam and I to end on at least okay terms because I didn't want to live my life without him being a part of it in some way.

The truth was, if I was going to get over Cameron, I needed him to tell me the truth. I needed him to stop doing the things that he was used to doing, to stop coming around like my boyfriend, to stop letting me try, to stop telling me he loved me.

I asked him countless times if he was seeing someone else. I told him not to hurt me more than he already had, but he insisted on keeping me around, and I just stayed.

My health was horrible. I was constantly at the doctors, and I even had a breast cancer scare. My mother underwent surgery. Just when I thought I had hit my lowest, my life got worse and worse. Everything was flipped upside down.

After my mother's surgery, I had called Cameron to help me take care of her. My entire family had work that day and my mom needed someone to be there with her because she was unable to walk.

He came to the rescue and spent the morning at my house taking care of my mother. That day Cameron had told my mom that we would be working things out with our relationship.

I had hope.

After that day, I knew that Cameron would come around. He loved my mother and respected my family. I wouldn't have believed Cameron was capable of hurting me more than I had already hurt myself, but that thought was shot down when I found out he was sleeping with and dating another girl while he was sleeping with me.

I couldn't understand how he could do this to me when he

knew what I had been dealing with. Cameron was my first and only, and the fact that he disrespected by cheating killed me inside. This was the ultimate betrayal.

I was officially done with Cameron. He was dead to me.

I found the girl on Twitter and got her number after direct messaging her. Her name was Cynthia.

I called her and explained to her the situation, and we devised a plan to meet up with Cam at the same time. Cameron and I were supposed to be meeting later that day, and I asked Cynthia to join us. She agreed and gave me her address to pick her up.

Like me, Cynthia had a horrible ex-boyfriend before Cameron who had hurt her and, just like me, she vowed to never be taken advantage of again.

Later that day, I picked Cynthia up from her house and drove to Hunter's, where Cameron had told me he would be. He, however, wasn't expecting me to come over. When I arrived at Hunter's, no one was there.

A few minutes passed, and Cameron's car pulled up in front of the house. Assuming that he realized that my car was also there, he tried to pull away, but Cynthia and I had decided that he wouldn't be getting away that easily.

We both jumped out of the car and blocked Cameron in. We marched over to the driver side of his car, Cynthia with two open bottles of water in hand. Cameron tried to roll up his window, but Cynthia stuck her arm through it, to stop it from closing. He rolled the window back down, and hopped out of the car.

We fussed, cursed, yelled, and told Cameron exactly what he was to us.

"You not shit!" Cynthia screamed before throwing the two bottles of water on Cameron.

I reached for his wrist and broke the bracelet that I had given him, and threw the bracelet that I had on my wrist at him.

Everything that I felt was coming out in this very moment.

I was truly broken and fed up. I didn't want Cam and I to end like this, but there was no other option.

~

Even after our altercation, I wanted back. I was so in love with him, but he made it quite clear that we would never get back together.

And two months later, he began dating Rebecca, just as I predicted he eventually would. She was the same girl he told me not to worry about. The same girl he swore he would never date.

And there it was.

I had lost my friend of six years. I lost the love of my life. I lost the person I gave my everything to.

I cried every night and put on a fake smile every day.

I cut off all my hair and changed the way I dressed. I got a sunflower tattooed on my shoulder to remind to keep my strength, to stay bright and appear unbroken, just like a sunflower, but nothing was working.

I wasn't getting any better.

I even went as far as to sleep with different people just to cover up the fact that I gave Cameron something that meant so much to me, something that I could never get back. I didn't want Cameron to be so special, so I gave the same gift that I had given him away to others.

I went to parties. I drank and smoked and went wild in front of his friends just to make sure it would get back to him.

I made a fool of myself on social media. I posted all my thoughts so he could know what I was thinking.

I made it look like I was having fun when, deep down inside, I was dead and he and everyone else knew it.

I had lost something great. Memories of us replayed in my head all the time. Everything reminded me of him. I didn't know how I would overcome, and how I would bounce back from this heartbreak. My breakup with Cameron was the hardest thing I ever had to deal with.

I hated myself for the decisions I made, and I hated Cameron for the decisions he made.

The day I pulled up on Cameron with Cynthia was the last time I actually spoke to him and it killed me inside.

I wasn't hurt because I lost my relationship. I was hurt because I lost a friend of so long. It hurt me to see that he let me beg, cry, and fight when all the while he had no true intentions of getting back together.

It killed me that everything was ripped away so fast, and I couldn't get it back.

Cameron seemed to have moved on quickly. He seemed to have bounced back from our breakup like it didn't affect him, and that hurt me even more.

My second heartbreak took a lot out of me.

It changed me.

Once again, I closed myself up, holding all of my feelings inside.

I never understood how people overcame these situations.

I was stuck. I watched him move on. I watched his love for me turn into hatred. I watched the person I fell in love with walk out of my life forever, and not once, not for a second did he look back.

I always wondered if he knew exactly how he made me feel. If he knew how much damage he had brought to my heart and mind.

I hated Cameron. I hated him because I loved him and couldn't imagine life without him. I hated him because I cared about him— his future and his well-being. Because I wanted him to be by my side, and he wasn't there. Because he hated me.

Most of all I hated him for being just like Bryant.

CHAPTER ELEVEN

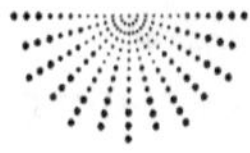

Love: something that must come within or from a spiritual place before it can be projected

It took me a while to realize that pretending to be okay was not going to be enough. It took me a while to see that getting drunk wasn't going to solve my problems, or that no matter how much I changed my hair, or smoked, I would never again be the girl that Cameron wanted. I had to realize that Cameron didn't care about my long text messages and my sad tweets along with my hopeless Snapchats of sad songs and faint memories.

It took me some time to accept the fact that it was time to find myself and move on. It was not easy for me.

As women, we are built to be strong. We are built to deal with challenges in life and we are built to overcome these challenges, but I was so tired of being strong. I had no more fight left in me. I hated that I had to overcome yet another disappointment.

"You can do it."

"It was his loss."

"You are too strong to let this affect you."

Everyone would say, but words didn't amount to what I was feeling inside.

Why did I have to be strong when he made me so weak? Why did I have to be the bigger person when he belittled me? Why did I have to walk away when I was giving him my biggest fight?

I didn't have the answers to these questions, but I knew that in order to get better, I didn't need the answers.

I was going down this dark path, and I honestly thought there was no turning back. I never thought I would come out on top, and I didn't believe that I could be better than I was before. I was in a tunnel with no light and no outlet. I thought this would be me for the rest of my life, but I didn't want it to be.

It wasn't until one day when I read my daily devotional that my life took a turn for the better.

I stared at my phone screen and whispered the Bible verse to myself. I read Bible verses every day. I never realized that most of the verses applied to me, and they would soon direct me to make a change in my life.

Luke 6:45 was my saving grace. The light in my tunnel, this verse changed my entire life.

"A good man brings good things out of the good stored up in his heart, and an evil man brings evil things out of the evil stored up in his heart. For the mouth speaks what the heart is full of," I read.

I realized that the person I was on the outside was not the person I was inside.

My heart was pure, my heart was caring, my heart was loving, and my heart was broken, but what my heart carried was not reflected on the outside.

On the outside I was a totally different person. I was rude, spiteful. I put myself up high because deep inside, I was so low. I pretended I didn't care about people's feelings and I liked to think that I was ruthless, but deep down, I wasn't. I cared too much. I loved too hard. I got attached too fast, and I fell too easy.

When I read this verse, it broke me down, and everything was realized. I knew my way out of this depression and what needed to be done to get over the breakup.

As teens and young adults, we get so caught up in the façade of having a perfect relationship. We see it on social media, in movies and TV shows, and we get so caught up in wanting that "love story" that we see, but we go about getting it the wrong way. In essence, we look for love in all the wrong places, and the first place we look is outside of ourselves.

I was so quick to give my love to someone else I forgot to give my love to the person that mattered the most—myself.

I found myself giving these guys all of me. I put my everything into all of my relationships—my love, my peace of mind, my happiness, my focus. I invested myself to the point that when they left, I had given them so much that I had nothing left.

I worked on the relationship and pushed for it and gave away my heart because I wanted to be loved. I wanted someone to love me. I wanted to feel loved, but how could I expect someone to love me when I didn't even love myself?

I didn't know how much self-love was worth. I wasn't aware that once I found self-love, no one would be able to take me back to that dark place that I found with Bryant and Cameron. I didn't have a clear understanding of what it meant to truly love myself, and loving myself turned out to be the biggest challenge I ever had to take on. I was unhappy with my hair, unhappy with my body, unhappy with my personality, but it wasn't because I was simply dissatisfied, it was because my past and all the things I went through made me think of myself on a lower level.

I didn't love the person I was because that person was not me.

Luke 6:45 did not just open my eyes, it also changed the person I was and the person I was soon to become.

Your heart reflects the person you are. The words you speak are words that reflect your heart. I chose to reflect the true me. I chose to turn over my new leaf, to show the world what God truly made.

Everything began to make sense. I realized that I shouldn't be malicious towards my exes. I shouldn't hate them. I shouldn't be mad at them for hurting me. My heart may have been broken, but it held so much more than pain.

My heartbreaks happened for a reason. They built me up and shaped me to be better. Yes, they hurt me and took me to a place where I thought I could not return from, but they also challenged me. I had to find my way out.

My change didn't come quickly, however. I stayed in my dark place for more than a year because I dwelled on my past. I cried spontaneously and lashed out and had suicidal thoughts for a year and a half. I threw myself to the wire and damaged myself more and more for a year and a half. I read old text messages and reached out to Cam to try to mend our friendship for a year and a half. I drove past his house, drove past his job, went to our favorite restaurants just to feel something that use to give my heart happiness for a year and a half. I even tried with different guys after Cam, but my heart was missing something. My heart continued to get hurt with these guys as well because they only wanted one thing. They had no intention of doing right by me.

I soon realized what my heart was yearning for what no man on this earth was capable of giving me.

It took me a year and a half to let go and put an end to this chapter to take on the next.

See, we are expected to just get over breakups, to forget about everything and just move on. We are told not to dwell on the past, but losing someone that made you so happy, that you gave so much of yourself to is not just something you can get over. You can't just throw away feelings. You can't just wake up one day and be okay.

But realization can help you through it.

When I realized what was missing, my life began. This was when I gave everything in me to one man that I knew would never let me down—this is when I gave it all to the God.

~

Happiness does not come from having a significant other. Happiness does not come from drugs and alcohol. Happiness does not come from negative attention. Happiness is determined by you. Your relationships and your friendships should not be the only reason you are happy. Happiness comes from within because love comes from within.

You must love yourself before you give yourself to someone else.

It was so hard trying to love myself when the world was giving me a thousand and one reasons why I shouldn't. I stopped caring about what people thought of me and spoke of me.

I put my worth in a higher power. I put my faith in God and, from that moment on, no one could tell me anything about myself —my life, my struggles, my happiness was between me and God. My Bible verses became my inspirations to love myself and be happy.

I began to share God with others and encouraged others to love themselves.

I finally realized that I had to be my own first love.

I soon came to understand that God was not punishing me. Everything that happened in my life only pulled me out and made me a stronger person, and I used my stories to guide others. I would be an outlet for others who were in the same dark place that I had been in, those who struggled with the same demons that I once fought.

I never understood what God was doing until I put complete faith in Him and what He was doing.

The truth of the matter is, heartbreak and loss is inevitable in this life, and we never truly understand why we are put in these situations. Some don't make it out. Overcoming the toxic views, overcoming the obstacles placed in front of you, and coming out on top is all better than letting the world break you down. I went from a narrow-minded girl who believed she had very little to offer, to heartbroken, to suicidal, to depressed, just to end up exactly where I needed to be—somewhere in the middle of losing the love of others and finding it within myself.

So, shout-out to my exes, shout-out to my heartbreak because without you I wouldn't be where God intended me to be.

CHAPTER TWELVE

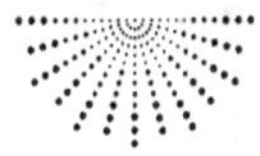

In the moment between relationships and constantly getting hurt, I was unaware of what God was trying to do with me. I didn't fully understand his plan. I was unsure of how all my pain and hurt was supposed to amount to something.

This book is not a bash fest. I'm not explaining how bad my exes hurt me, but how I found an outlet for me to share with the world what many women are afraid to tell. Going through these heartbreaks, I learned how to cope with pain and find love in something more important than a physical relationship. God wasn't punishing me like I thought he was. He wasn't *destroying* my happiness. He was *creating* my happiness.

This message is to inspire girls to find purpose in themselves, to love themselves when it seems that no one else does, and to believe even when it seems that they have nothing to believe in.

Life isn't about loving someone. It's about loving yourself and watching everything else grow from that.

Purposeful Millennials Publishing Co. publishes books that empower the millennial generation. We help millennial authors publish their literary work. Our mission is to empower the millennial generation to walk in their purpose through book publishing. In an environment where everything we do is purposeful, we believe that we can be a guiding tool to shift this generation for the better. We are a Christian-based company and are guided by the word of God.